Sense of Place:

Stories about Community and Belonging

Nerelie Teese

ISBN: 978-1-923163-25-6 (Paperback)

 A catalogue record for this work is available from the National Library of Australia

Cover Design: Nerelie Teese and Clark & Mackay
Format and Typeset: Clark & Mackay
Published by Nerelie Teese and Clark & Mackay

Proudly printed in Australia by Clark & Mackay

Contents

Morning

As the rolling thunder and forked lightning from the overnight storm becomes nothing more than a sleepy memory, the sky begins losing its depth of darkness in the east. Perched high on branches or snuggled safely in their nests, birds of all sizes begin to stir. Trembling with anticipation, their little bodies shake as they fluff their feathers in readiness for this brand-new day and the many miles they will fly.

The creatures of the night begin to slow down from their feeding, mating, and social frenzy. Large eyes begin to droop, pupils narrow, and breathing slows in preparation for the coming day of rest. Quietly, softly, tiredly, they burrow, curl, or snuggle in safety—hiding from the sharp bright eyes of predators who may seek them during daylight.

Night slowly fades, yet the moon still hangs low in the western sky, refusing to retreat from its canvas. While it is not quite sunrise, the new dawn creeps over the horizon, across the wide-open plains towards the small town nestled amongst and around the narrow strip of ancient forest lining the slow-moving river.

Somewhere, on one of the sleeping streets, a dog barks. The rumble of a garage door is quickly joined by the starting of a car engine. Reversing lights glow through semi-darkness as the vehicle backs off the driveway onto the road. The garage door rumbles to a close as the dark shape of a fully grown cat leaps up onto the fence, causing the dog to bark once more.

"Bloody cat," mutters the driver as she catches a glimpse of its sleek silhouette in the beam of her headlights. As if hearing her, the cat flicks its tail as casually as a teenager gives the finger to a mate before leaping down from the fence and gracefully stalking homewards. Once there, the driver knows, it will curl up on the veranda in the first warm rays of sunlight, looking deceptively innocent when its human opens the front door to collect the newspaper after the paper boy's wild throw from astride his shiny black and red six-speed pushbike.

Shaking her head and smiling, she lifts the travellers' cup of coffee to her eager lips then indicates the right turn into the small town's business centre. Just a few hundred metres along, she indicates again before turning into the narrow laneway leading to the small private car park.

Automatically scanning the fenced-in area before picking up her bag and coffee, she turns off the headlights and removes the keys from the ignition. Selecting the building's door key, she clicks the lock on her car and walks towards the back door of the bakery. Her bakery. The town's bakery. And she smiles again, anticipating the inviting aromas of her freshly baked bread, croissants and other delights that will soon waft up and down the street, enticing other early risers to come in for a morning treat.

She unlocks the door and enters, automatically turning on the lights and putting the keys in her pocket. Then she places her bag on the small rickety desk and reaches for the freshly laundered apron she'd hung up in readiness the afternoon before. Happiness fills her heart as she begins work knowing, for now, this is what she wants and is meant to do—feed and nurture others for their essential roles in this small community she loves so much. Her community. Her town.

Meanwhile, on the other side of town, the council depot swings into action. External lights flood its car park, reflections shining in the puddles left by the storm. Gates are unlocked. Voices talk softly or call out eagerly, sometimes with a burst of laughter as the workday begins. The road crews come together for their day's briefing, looking forward to what some of the townsfolk might carelessly call a day of doing nothing much at all.

However, each driver knows that the work done grading the kilometres of gravel backroads, repairing potholes in bitumen roads, slashing roadside grass, and checking bridges, culverts, and other infrastructure adds to the wellbeing and safety of their community. Further along from the depot, the town's garbage truck comes to life as its driver swings up into the cabin to begin his essential role in supporting the health and cleanliness of his township.

Diagonally opposite the council yards, on top of the small rise fondly known as the Hill, the little hospital also begins welcoming the new day. The night-shift nurses make one last check of their patients, silently giving thanks that none have soundlessly slipped away in the time between night and morning when human life and spirit are traditionally at their lowest.

Quietly and efficiently, their sleeping charges are checked, monitored, and accounted for. The night-shift nurses hear the hum of engines as the morning crew arrives in the staff car park. They listen to that moment of silence before car doors close and voices call out greetings, followed by the gentle slap of rubber soles moving across bitumen to concrete pathways and the gathering of their colleagues at the hospital's entry. Another day of hospital routine is about to begin. The night-shift nurses relax, knowing soon they'll be heading home.

Further out of the little town, farm dogs yawn before standing up and stretching then moving to their favourite place to squat or cock a leg in anticipation of their daily routine. They hear their humans moving around inside the house, see lights come on and move to greet the men and women who make their doggy lives complete. Knowing their working skills bring pleasure and satisfaction to their people has tails wagging, ears pricking, and doggy lips smiling, looking forward to whatever work, fun, and adventures the day will bring.

In nearby yards, horses whinny their soft greeting to this new day before rippling their hides and then joyfully cantering along and around their purposefully fenced enclosure. At the far end of the paddock, they disdainfully nicker at the docile cattle already grazing in the soft morning's light. Very few of the cattle bother acknowledging their presence. Those that do lift their large heads, dark bovine eyes giving a disinterested glance before softly blowing a gentle whoosh of air through thick lips in a subtle sign of careless disrespect.

From an overhanging branch, a kookaburra cackles its delight at the scene below, enjoying this communication between species. Triggered by that first outburst of happiness, others reply, setting off a chain of laughter that echoes across the paddocks causing kangaroos and wallabies to look up and around, ears flicking to sense any nearby threats or danger. Hearing and sensing nothing to fear at this moment, some gently scratch their tummies while others return to carefully picking at the long grass and budding wildflowers scattered in the damp shade beneath ancient gum trees. The harsh cawing of a crow disturbs the silence as the despised carrion-eater scans the earth below for easy pickings.

While dawn has gradually introduced the beginning of this new day, suddenly, like a spotlight piercing the night, the sun bursts over the horizon, carelessly flinging its heat overall. On this summer morning, there will be no gentle warming of the forest, fields, and plains.

The slow spring warming of earth and sky is nothing more than a fond memory for the creatures who look up and around, searching for clouds to gently drift between them and the scorching golden orb on its long, dry journey to the opposite horizon before the soothing embrace of twilight and peaceful respite from another Australian midsummer day.

Between gently sloping banks, the river slowly drifts south, its waters sparkling as beams of sunlight reflect off its ripples. This calm scene is suddenly broken by the town's kids racing to be the first to dive-bomb into its smooth inviting surface. Echoes of calls, yells, and shrieks of laughter float up and across to the adults already at work or on their way to the busyness of another day. They stop and smile, remembering their own days spent in this rite of passage before time snatched away the freedom of their youth and led to the responsibilities of adulthood and their roles in this community they work for and love.

And in that quiet pause of reflection and reminiscence, they smell the tempting aromas wafting through the air and, almost as one, move towards its source to indulge in a little taste of pleasure from their bakery before beginning their day of routine and service in their small country town. This is their place. Their home. Their future.

Midday

During what she hoped was just the usual mid-morning lull between customers, Debbie wiped the already clean and shiny countertop and then moved to the indoor tables, giving them a quick tidy before going out onto the footpath. The three al fresco tables just needed a wipe to remove the light layer of dust stirred up by passing cars, school buses, cattle trucks, motorbikes, and the occasional grain truck driving through town. After making slight adjustments to the small vases holding flowers and greenery cut from her garden the afternoon before, Debbie stepped back and admired them, allowing herself a small smile of pride and satisfaction.

Then, lifting her gaze and turning around, she gave action to the real reason she'd stepped out of her small welcoming café. "Take-a-Break" was her dream come true. And now as she looked up and down the main street and business centre of her little country town, she gave a sigh of relief. Not an empty car park in sight. While that wasn't a guarantee of a busy lunchtime, it was a good indicator that, around midday, she and Stu, her tall, good-humoured, first-class cook and her two casual waitstaff would be kept busy for a couple of hours before the next little lull that led to what Debbie thought of as the "milkshake rush", when the high school kids called in to chill out on their way home.

It is predictable, kind of, she thought, grinning as she heard the back screen door bang shut. *Yep, there's Elly.* Giving a last look up and down the long street, which really was just an urbanised and commercial section of the interstate highway, she walked back inside.

"Good morning, boss; morning Stu," came the lighthearted Irish lilt from Debbie's latest and favourite backpacker. "There's a touch of autumn in the air this morning." The auburn-haired young woman grinned, her green eyes twinkling in delight. "Sure, and it won't be long before we can't hear the kids yahooing and splashing in the river early in the mornings. Do they still swim there in the afternoons this time o' the year?"

"Some do," Stu replied. "Although it's usually just the older boys—they've got to keep up their tough-man image," he said with a chuckle. "But the girls will be there as well, sunning themselves like little lizards, keeping their tans as long as they can."

Debbie nodded in agreement. "That's right, Elly. You might like to give it a go one afternoon, too. This time of year, your beautiful Irish skin shouldn't burn like it did earlier in summer, and there are some nice little spots on the riverbank that are perfect for a rug, a book, and an apple or two. The seniors"—referring to the older high school students—"would love to see you down there with them. You know how much they adore you." She smiled as the pink flush crept up Elly's neck and into her face.

"Well, now, Debbie," Elly replied, "that's a lovely thing to hear and those kids are sweeties, I'll think about it. But," she continued hesitantly, "what about those dreadful snakes of yours?" She shuddered. "I just couldn't bear the thought of seeing another one … those little evil, beady eyes. Uurgh." She shook her head as she reached out for her freshly ironed Take-a-Break apron.

"You'd be okay, Elly, love," Stu said, looking at her worried face. "That was just a bit of bad luck when that Joe Blake curled itself up on your back step. It was probably just soaking up some sun, and I bet it just shit itself when you started screaming at it to go away." Even Elly laughed a little at his description of the fright she'd had on that hot summer morning a few weeks ago. "Stu," she reminded him, "you know I was terrified. I'd never even seen a live snake before and there the bloody thing was all curled up like a huge coil of rope on my back step. And then it lifted its head and those evil beady eyes glared at me as if I shouldn't have even been there. It's my granny flat. I'm the one paying the rent. And I don't want to share any part of it with any slimy, slithering—" She broke off and moved towards the coffee machine. "Oh, good morning to you, Constable Bill. Your regular morning tea supplies?" She smiled, setting out six take-away cups.

"Yes please, Elly," his deep voice replied. "Three flat whites, two cappuccinos, and a skinny latte with the Anzac biscuits today, thanks." He nodded at Debbie and Stu. "G'day. How's it going Stu, Debbie?" He smiled at them before turning his attention back to Elly.

"They're not slimy, you know," he said, grinning as she stopped working the machine with a surprised look at him."Huh?" Elly asked.

"Snakes. They're not slimy," the policeman replied as he winked at Stu and Debbie.

With a chuckle, Debbie moved towards the small back room she grandly called her office. "Can't wait to see how you get yourself out of that one, Bill," she said, picking up the small bucket of cleaning items and moving towards the restrooms. "Elly's still getting over the fright of her up-close-and-personal encounter. Not that I blame her," she quickly added, looking sympathetically at Elly. "I don't like the things either. But Bill is right, you know—they're not slimy. They're sort of smooth, if you can bring yourself to touch one. Lizards are much easier to put up with." She smiled, thinking of Bluey, the old blue-tongue lizard that lived in her backyard and gratefully ate the snails she plucked out of her flower beds for him.

"Have a good day, Bill," she continued as she went into the restrooms to make sure they were respectable for the midday rush she felt sure was coming. Knowing that her clean, tidy, and fresh-smelling toilets were part of the attraction for her regular customers, as well as the delight of people passing through who didn't want to walk the block and a half to the public toilets and whatever condition they might be in once they got there, was incentive for Debbie to do the three-times-daily "dunny duty", as she and her staff referred to it amongst themselves.

"Enjoy the coffee and the Anzacs," she called out, enjoying the rich coffee aroma wafting through the café as the restroom door closed behind her. Just a few minutes later, with a look of satisfaction at her work, Debbie finished polishing the mirror in the ladies', acknowledging that the girls and women who used her facilities were so appreciative of this attractive comfort they often wiped any splashes of water off the basin and benchtop, leaving it almost as clean as Debbie did.

"Good morning, Gemma," Debbie called out to her junior staff member as she walked back into her office. Gemma, who was back in town for her uni holidays, had arrived nicely ahead of her shift as she always did. "Street parking's full, or it was earlier, so I think we'll be nice and busy today. Stu will tell you today's specials and we'll all have a little taste so we can give our recommendations if we're asked.

"As you know, it doesn't matter if we give different recs, as long as we can answer any queries honestly. I know I've said this before, but I've never forgotten the worried look on that young waiter's face up on the Gold Coast when I asked which of the specials he'd recommend. The poor thing." She shook her head at the memory. "That's when I decided that, when I opened my own place, everyone would be able to give their own recommendations—even if it's different from mine. After all ..." She waited and then they chorused, "our tastebuds are all as different as we are," and the close-knit team smiled at each other.

"Okay, Gemma," Debbie continued, "if you can get more cutlery and serviettes ready for the midday rush, we'll be right to go. *And yes,* she said to herself, *here they come.* "Maisie, Betty, and Lorna," she cheerfully greeted the three ladies who'd walked in together. "Isn't this a lovely day, and don't you all look swish? Love your new do, Betty; it really suits you. Your usual table, ladies?" She walked with them to the window table. "Is Jane joining you today?" she asked as she pulled out the chairs for the lovely group of octogenarians. Carefully, but without fussing too much, she made sure each one was comfortable, placing two small jugs of water—easier for older hands to lift and pour—with four glasses on the table and then smiling and nodding at Gemma, who brought over the menus, each one attractively embellished with delicate violas that Debbie had picked and pressed from her garden.

"Thank you, dear," Maisie said, smiling at the young waitress before gently elbowing her. "C'mon, your boss isn't watching—let me give my beautiful Gemma a kiss." The old lady smiled as she hugged her beloved granddaughter before lightly kissing her cheek, knowing it wouldn't matter one little bit if Debbie was watching. "It's so good to see you, darling girl," she whispered as Gemma straightened up and smiled lovingly at her grandmother and the group fondly known as the town's "Grannies".

"It's good to see you too, Nan," she replied, "and all of you." She nodded at Betty and Lorna. "You know, it makes our day," she pretended to whisper confidentially, "when our Grannies come in to catch up. Let me know when you're ready to order. I'm sure Stu will pop over to see his sweethearts soon." With a gentle caress of her grandmother's shoulder, Gemma walked back to her cutlery duty, where she could keep an eye on the tables and the door.

While there didn't seem to be any rhyme or reason for it, suddenly the little café appeared full and almost overflowing. Elly was kept busy at the coffee machine as the take-away line built up and Gemma and Debbie moved gracefully around and between the tables, taking orders and holding short, friendly conversations with customers.

Stu appeared almost dancer-like as he moved from the stovetop to the oven and the bench, efficiently and attractively plating orders that were also beginning to build up. Once all the tables were filled and orders taken, Debbie moved into the kitchen to help him. Knowing that they worked well together made it easy for her to assist him, and she usually carried the dishes out to the tables so she could chat, however briefly, to her customers.

Looking around, Debbie wondered yet again if it was time to add to her enthusiastic team of staff. She moved to one side and watched Gemma interacting with the customers: a smile here, a wave there, a cheerful comment and a laugh as she cleared tables. *Yes*, Debbie thought, *if I upskill Gemma and she shares the coffee-making with Elly in busy times like this, that'd be another pair of hands behind the counter, and we could easily use another junior for table service and cleaning up. Or maybe,* she thought, looking at the harried young mum who'd just joined the takeaway line, *maybe a part-time senior. One who I know needs the money and who I already know can do the work.*

"Hey, Jenny," she said happily to the young woman as she placed her order with Elly. "How's it all going? You well? Kids going along okay?"

"Yes, thanks, Debbie," came the soft reply. "It's been a busy morning and I'm in need of this before I go home and get stuck back into it. Mum's got the baby while I do the shopping, the twins are at kindy, and the washing machine should have finished before I get home to do the next lot. You know how it is—busy, busy, busy." Jenny looked around at the crowded tables. "Yep," she continued, "it sure looks like you know how it is; you're flat out, too." She passed Elly a five-dollar note, nodded her thanks, said goodbye, and left.

Elly had been carefully watching the exchange between the young mum and her boss. "She'd be good, you know, Debbie," Elly said softly. "We're getting busier and busier, and I know you're thinking about opening up the back as a bit of a courtyard. Jenny, or someone like her, would be a good addition if that all goes ahead. Just saying." She smiled as Debbie looked at her in amazement.

"Am I that easy to read?"

"Only because you talk about things with us, and you're careful and thoughtful about your plans. Just saying, you know." Elly smiled again. "And you know my lips are sealed until you want to speak about it all. Or even if you don't," she added with a laugh.

Slowly, people finished eating and left. Many of them pretended to groan with full tummies as they paid, smiled, and walked away saying they wouldn't need to eat again for two or three days. That always made Debbie and Stu smile, mainly because they'd carefully worked out the serving sizes and most plates always came back empty. They'd both agreed that for the café to be sustainable and economical, there had to be minimal food waste. And in a very short time, they had reached their goal of less than ten percent of plates having any food left on them. Between the worm farm and the compost bins, this waste was always taken care of, and Debbie's flower beds gained the benefit.

Having waved goodbye to the Grannies earlier, Gemma filled the window table three times with new customers before the midday crowd thinned. Some were regulars, but others were travellers passing through who had been attracted by the cheerful table settings on the footpath and then managed to find a car park. Now the café had quietened, Gemma passed their praise and compliments onto Debbie and the team. She took her phone from her pocket and quickly looked at Take-a-Break's Facebook page. "Yep, they did just what they said they were going to," she said, passing the phone to Debbie. "Look at their lovely comments. No wonder the word's getting around to people who are going up and down the highway. This kind of comment just draws people in, and how about this about the toilets? 'Worth driving all this way just for the clean, welcoming ladies' room'. And they said they'd be back in on their way home. They live somewhere up on the Darling Downs, a couple of hours out from Toowoomba. There's a farm fest the other side of Narranderra that they're going to, so they'll be telling others about us; just you wait and see. There's a bit of travel time between towns out here and the road safety message about having a break every couple of hours seems to be getting through to drivers."

"I love the way people tell you things, Gemma," Stu said, looking thoughtfully at the young woman. "You're so interested in people and what they're doing. Fancy getting all that in between seating them and taking their orders. You're not bad at this, love, are you?" He beamed down at her. "Well," she replied, "they were nice people. They said nice things about us and our food, so it was easy to talk to them. And, Elly," she said, looking at the barista, "they loved your coffee—said it was the best they'd had on this trip. So they'll be back," she finished confidently.

"That's fantastic, Gemma," Debbie said delightedly. "Now, Stu, you're about to knock off soon, so we'll get the kitchen area cleaned up. Girls, if you can take care of the rest of it, you'll be able to leave on time, Elly—and Gemma, you and I should be right for this afternoon's "milkshake rush" before you finish up. Then you'll be able to get stuck into that assignment you mentioned yesterday and have the rest of your break to recover from your studies. We all know how hard you're working at uni. It's not only Maisie and the Grannies who are proud of what you're doing. So, everyone, let's get the rest of this day underway." With that, Debbie and Stu moved into the kitchen, and Elly and Gemma busied themselves at the counter and resetting the tables.

As Gemma looked after the café during the little lull, Debbie busied herself with the books in her office. Going back over the last three months' figures, she nodded happily at what she saw. "Another couple of months like these and I just might be able to extend out the back, get Stu to add to the menu or change it, and see if Jenny would like to pick up three or four days work during the week. Hmm …" Then she went right back into the previous twelve months' figures.

It's looking good, she thought to herself. Sipping from the still-hot mug of afternoon coffee she allowed herself, Debbie reflected on her plans for Take-a-Break. From opening her dream café, she'd known that if everything did go to plan, then she'd move to weekend openings—*Ticked that box,* she thought happily.

Soon, she'd start looking into planning the extension into the courtyard, and then there'd be the new Friday night openings. *Jenny, or whoever, won't be enough,* she realised. And almost automatically, she glanced at her watch, knowing that school would soon be over and her "milkshake rush" would start.

"Gemma, if you want to take a quick break, I'll look after things. It won't be long now and the high schoolers will be in. Quick," she said with a smile, "what'll it be today? Choc, caramel, or strawberry?" Their flavour-of-the-day tipping competition had become part of the afternoon's routine and, at times, they'd wondered if the high-schoolers knew about it, because sometimes the popular flavours might stay the same day after day, and then they could chop and change like the infamous Melbourne weather. Suddenly, or so it seemed, the last of the chattering teenagers left, calling out a cheery "See ya tomorrow" as they headed out the door on their way home.

"Well, that's that for today, Gemma." Debbie smiled at her as Gemma stacked the tea towels in the washing basket.

"Off you go, see if you can grab some of this lovely afternoon weather before you chain yourself to the computer, and I'll see you tomorrow morning."

"No worries, Debbie," she replied. "But what about you? Why don't you knock off now instead of working until well after dark? Why don't you get some of that quality time you're always advising Stu and us about? You never seem to stop, and we don't want you to wear yourself out."

"Oh, Gemma, that's so thoughtful of you, but I don't see this as work. Not really. This is what I've wanted to do since I first backpacked through Europe when I was at uni. Just seeing what a café like this means to a small community opened my eyes to what life can be all about. Those little cafés in Greece, Italy, and France showed me that people will always need or want somewhere local to catch up, chat, drink, and eat. And that's what I decided I wanted to do. I worked in a couple of them, thinking I was just getting the vibe, thinking I was seeing how they worked. But I got so much more. Some of my former employers still email me, and that's why I love having backpackers in here. It's a bit like paying it back but, who knows, it might also trigger something about small communities and how they work for them, and I think Elly really gets it. Some of the others we've had here didn't. And that's okay, too. And that's why this isn't work, hard work for me. So, thanks for your kind words and thoughts, but I do get the lovely afternoons at weekends when we close earlier. So, off you go now; scoot! Go and work on that law degree of yours, and then when that's done and dusted, maybe you'll think about working in a community like this, too. Goodness knows we could use a solicitor just like you here. See you tomorrow."

And then, with the little outdoor tables stored back inside and the front door locked, Debbie looked around her little patch of paradise, smiled, stretched, and went back into her office to reimagine her plans for the new courtyard extension.

Moonlight

Her excitement had slowly been building for days and this afternoon she could feel it beginning to peak. Carefully, thoughtfully, mindfully, she allowed herself time to reflect, just once more, on all the planning and coordination that had gone into the action that would soon take place.

The original thought had been different; she could accept that as she looked around her. Yes, she admitted, it had been quite a few years ago, but the idea had never gone away. That original fleeting thought, that incredible idea, had sat in the back of her mind, just simmering away like a pot of her beloved grandmother's pea-and-ham soup on the old combustion stove in the farmhouse kitchen so long ago. The longer the soup simmered, the more delicious it became. And so had her idea. Or so she believed. And the longer her idea simmered, the more she knew it had to happen. She felt the universe was demanding it. She knew she wanted it to happen. And, she often thought, so too would her dearest friend Anna.

When she finally found the confidence to talk to Anna about her idea, Anna's enthusiastic support confirmed her belief in the grace and beauty of the idea and its adventure, although, after a few glasses of rich, red wine, voicing her idea made it sound more like one of their juvenile boarding school schemes than the brilliance sparked by glimpsing the full moon rising between the far-off mountain peaks of the Great Dividing Range.

Nervously, she cautiously looked around once more. Knowing that earlier she'd scouted the area, to carefully ensure that she wouldn't be seen or heard by any unexpected passers-by, boosted her confidence. Confidence, she felt, that she would need if this really was going to happen.

However, that sneaky little voice in the back of her mind kept whispering that it wouldn't matter if she chickened out. *There'll be another time,* she could hear it murmuring. *Another time, another place. You don't have to do this now. Anna won't mind; she'll understand.* Ruthlessly stomping on the voice and its whispering, she glanced up and around once more. The twilight lingered. While the sun had slowly lowered itself beyond the distant skyline, its influence remained. As yet, the evening star hadn't appeared. *Hours yet,* the murmuring continued, *There's still time to ring Anna and call it off...* "For goodness' sake," she said aloud. "You know you want to do this, you know the time is right, and you know this is the right place. Just go and get ready." With that, she laughed. "Yes, I'll go and get ready right now. Because, tonight, at last, after all this time, this is really going to happen. Toughen up, princess, and go and get ready." With a slight shake of her head and one last careful look around, she moved back onto the veranda and into the house.

Once inside, she went straight to the computer. Knowing this wasn't necessary but using it as something positive to pass time and steady her mind and nerves, she touched the key that would take her to the bookmarked site. Taking a deep breath, she watched the screen and mirrored every move, focusing her mind on each stage, each breath that would help her succeed later.

Once finished, she went into the kitchen and poured cool mineral water over a freshly sliced piece of lemon, added a mint leaf picked from the pot on the windowsill, and then casually dropped two ice cubes into the tall sapphire-coloured glass. Another deep calming breath, and she moved back out to the veranda, noting that now the sky was beginning to darken. In the east, there was a faint glow of light bathing the horizon, and high above her, the first stars were starting to glimmer.

Slowly sipping her drink, she focused her attention on her senses, identifying the night-scented jasmine's perfume drifting on the evening's warm breeze that gently caressed her skin and hair. The warning call of nearby plovers almost covered the hoots from the mopoke that she knew lived two blocks away in a tall eucalypt tree. She swallowed, enjoying the refreshing aftertaste of mint and lemon. Her bare feet seemed to be absorbing the last of the day's warmth from the veranda's boards.

Almost statue-like, she stood and waited. Now calm, a sense of peace descended over her mind and body. Yes. She could feel the commitment surging through her. Tonight, after all this time, it would finally happen. She finished her drink, flicking what remained of the ice cubes onto the lawn, and walked back inside, placing the glass on the sparkling clean sink. Through the window she could see the night slowly creeping across her backyard, its darkness intensifying almost with every breath she took.

And then, as if it had leapt joyfully up and over the horizon, the full moon was above the skyline. Beaming at her. Glowing like a beacon guiding her to the right time and place. Her smart watch vibrated. Glancing down, she saw Anna's message. She grinned. Anna hadn't—wouldn't—let her down. They were in this together. Even though more than fifteen hundred kilometres separated them, they were doing this together.

Taking another deep breath, just as she knew Anna would be doing, she stepped off the veranda and moved to her yoga mat spread out on the grass, bathed in the glow of the full moon. Mindfully, she stepped onto the mat. One more deep breath and she was truly committed.

And subtly savouring every movement, she slowly undressed. The feeling of freedom was overwhelming as she gently removed each item of clothing and carefully let it fall to the ground. Then, standing there, in the glory of her nakedness and the embrace of the full moon, feeling the feminine energy pulsing through her veins and with a heightened awareness of her innate self, she reached upwards and outwards to gather and embrace energy from the universe.

As she began the graceful, ancient tai chi movements, a small part of her mind whispered gleefully, *Yes, you're doing it. You knew you would. And this is so very good.* And then, with full control over her mind and body, she gave herself up to the movements she enjoyed and had practised for so many years. The art of tai chi. Along with her long-held dream of doing this naked. Under the gentle, loving light of a full moon. Later that night, as she and Anna described their experiences, each enjoying a glass of rich, red wine, Anna voiced her envy. After all, while Anna had also done tai chi in the light of the full moon, she had been barefoot on the soft sand of a well-lit public beach and her being naked had never been part of the plan.

Riverbank

I've always loved this place—my place on the riverbank. It's my spot. Always has been, since I was a little girl and came here with my grandma, Nanna, to this place. Right here to this very spot. Of course, it'd been her place, her spot, first. But she shared it with me. She shared it with the rest of the family, too, but it's always been a special place for her and now for me.

Nanna used to talk about all the times she'd spent here when she was a young girl. She, her sisters and brothers, their cousins, their friends—they'd all meet here after school or at weekends to swim, to play, to fish or yabby, to yarn. As I grew older, I liked imagining the generations of Aboriginal children that would have done the same as us, Nanna, her son—my pa—and me, long before our family ever came to this area. But her childhood hours in this place were much shorter than mine. Being one of the eldest girls in her family, she'd have to hurry home, dragging the little ones behind her, to get her jobs done before dark.

"There was no electricity in those days," she'd say over and over. "And no flushing toilets, either. We had a sort of short, long-drop shelter over near the trees. I never knew how much I hated it—feared it, even—until the new septic toilets came and Dad put one at the back of the washhouse. They weren't called laundries then," she'd say with a laugh. Nanna would laugh even more as she described that last twilight rush out to the dunny before bedtime.

"We had to watch out for snakes—those bloody tiger snakes and the browns. God, I still hate snakes. And spiders. Those great big huntsman spiders. Some of them looked big enough to eat you. Well, to a scared little girl in the half-dark they did. But the thought of redbacks hiding in there was much worse. They were smaller and you wouldn't be able to see them in the dark of the dunny. And"—here she'd reach out and tickle me with spider-like hand movements—"every year when we'd go back to school, one of the bigger kids always had a story about some poor bloke getting bitten on the bum by a redback when he went out to the dunny in the dark. Of course"—she'd get thoughtful at this part of the story—"we never met anyone who had been bitten on the bum by a redback or anything else. But we'd always run home that afternoon to tell Mum and Dad.

When all of us were little, Dad would go out and make a big show of checking the dunny for redbacks and other scary things. But as we got older, he'd just grin and tell us to be careful. But the little ones would be so scared that us older ones would take it in turns to check it out before dark. We only had to do that for a couple of weeks, though. They'd soon forget about it, and the bigger kids would come out with new scary stories. Urban myths, I suppose they'd be called these days. I know I've told you the one about the swaggie—" She'd pause, waiting for me to ask her to tell me again. And I always did. And she always repeated it.

"Well, it was Billy Smith who told us on the first day back at school after Christmas and New Year. We had a new teacher that year. He was sort of young-ish and had been shot in the war. Think he'd fought somewhere in Europe—the Western Front, I think we heard it was. He never talked about it, and we were all told not to ask him about it. I remember he hated storms. If it looked like a thunderstorm was brewing, he'd send us all home early. We liked that. As long as we got home before the storm, that was. When I got older and understood more, I wondered if he knew the thunder would upset him. I've heard that some thunderstorms can sound like the battlefield. Poor bloke. Anyway, this first day back at school, we've got this new teacher and kids everywhere. Parents didn't take their kids to school back then. The kids just went. Grabbed a bit of bread and cheese, maybe an apple if they were lucky, and took themselves off to school. Of course, when there was a mob of kids with them, that made it easier for the young ones. By the time we got into town, near the school, we'd have ten maybe a dozen in our group, just walking along together. Unless we were running late, and then we'd be belting along that road. You didn't want to be late to school. Boy, you'd cop it if you were late.

"But the older kids, mostly the girls, they'd help the little kids get sorted and that helped the teacher, too. The big girls would line up the new kids, the first-year kids, stand them in line, and then the other kids would sort themselves out behind the littlies in their grades. We worked out there were nearly sixty kids at that little school with just the one teacher. And most of us turned out alright. We could all read and write and do sums and arithmetic. And poetry. Oh, how I loved poetry. 'The Wreck of the Hesperus', that was one of my favourites. I used to know it word for word and Dad would get me to recite it every Christmas. I loved doing it, too, until the year I heard Uncle Hec say, 'Oh no, here comes the bloody Hesperus again.' Well, I fixed the old sourpuss. I learnt a new one for the next Christmas, 'The Highwayman', and didn't that liven things up a bit. The oldies all connected it to Ned Kelly and there were arguments left, right, and centre about him and his gang." She'd always grin as she described that.

"But anyway, back to Billy Smith and his story about the swaggie." Here she'd peer at whoever was there as if to check they knew what a swaggie was. All we had to do was smile and nod and she'd pick her story back up again.

"Billy Smith said it all happened the night of the big storm. By crikey, that had been a big storm. Lightning cracking and flashing, thunder booming and crashing, and rain. Boy, did it rain that night. And the wind. I remember Dad was worried part of the roof might lift and there was nothing he could do. There was no way Mum would let him go outside to check and see what was happening. He would have had to take a kerosene lantern—*Tilley lanterns,* we called them—and that would have left us with just one in the kitchen with a couple of candles. So he had to stay inside with us.

"Well, Billy Smith told us that that night, a swaggie turned up at one of the outlying farmhouses. Right out on the plains, they were, with nothing and no-one around for miles. And just as the storm was working itself up into a real fury, he knocked on the door. Scared the living daylights out of the family. A dad, mum, and two little kids. Oh, and a couple of dogs. They were all sheltering inside together.

"There was no way anyone could be left outside in that storm. And they had their dogs in there with them, so they didn't want their animals outside, either. So the swaggie comes inside, into the house with the family. Then, three days after the storm, their closest neighbour called in to see how they'd managed. And he found them all … dead. The father, the mother, the two children, and the dogs. All dead. Billy Smith said finding the family like that sent the neighbour mad. There was nothing he could do. It sent him mad, Billy said. And he fled across the plains instead of going back to his place or coming into town to get the police.

"Well, that was what Billy Smith told all the kids at school on that first day back. We were all terrified. Couldn't get home to our parents quick enough. That poor new teacher. His very first day, and he was surrounded by hysterical kids. He asked what had happened, why were the children all upset, and Juney Cooper told him—she was one of the older girls, and I don't think she liked Billy Smith much. So, Mr Thompson called all the older kids into the schoolroom and asked the rest of us to please sit in the shade and wait for just a few minutes.

"Most of us were good kids and used to doing what we were told. Being asked without being told to or yelled at was a bit different, and I remember we looked at him, looked at each other, and just went and sat down in the shade. Then most of the big kids came out and spoke to us; they said Mr Thompson was coming out in a minute and that the story Billy Smith had told us was nothing more than that: a great big bad story to scare us and spoil everyone's first day at school. But Mr Thompson was clever. He'd sent two of the bigger boys over to the gaolhouse to get the sergeant.

"Juney Cooper settled us all down; she had us singing songs and counting, but we were all watching Mr Thompson. He came over and smiled at all of us and then said that we would be getting a special visitor and to please keep singing because it sounded so lovely, and he was looking forward to teaching us some new songs. Then he walked over to the gate—well, it wasn't really a gate, it was more of a gap in the fence at the front of the school—and just stood there, waiting. Then we saw the sergeant coming across the gravel road and some of the younger ones started crying again. But Juney and the other girls hushed them and kept them singing. The sergeant and Mr Thompson talked for a couple of minutes and the sergeant started looking really cross. Then Mr Thompson asked all of us to stand in formation. Well, we didn't have a clue what that meant. The sergeant coughed and asked us all to line up. That made sense to us, so we lined up in our grades. Then Mr Thompson introduced the sergeant to us. I thought that was funny, because we all knew who he was. He even had kids at the school. Mr Thompson said he'd had a report of a very bad story being told to the students and that had upset everyone. He then asked the sergeant if he'd heard this very bad story. 'No, Mr Thompson, I haven't heard anything about it until just now,' he replied. 'Do you know where this very bad story came from?'

"Mr Thompson said that he'd only heard it this morning himself and that was when Juney Cooper told him why all the children were upset. The sergeant asked Juney to come out and tell him what she knew. She was sitting across from me, and I saw her take a big breath. And I saw her look at Billy Smith, and he looked away. Juney stood up and walked over to the sergeant. I couldn't hear what they said, but I did see the sergeant give her his handkerchief. Then she wiped her face and came and sat down again.

"The sergeant called Billy Smith out to the front. He spoke to Billy and Mr Thompson and then asked Billy's brother Fred to come out. The sergeant took Billy and Fred to the gaolhouse. Mr Thompson asked us all to stand up. He said that if anyone needed to go to the toilet or to get a drink to do that before lining up to go inside.

"Some of the kids did; the rest of us just stood there. We didn't understand what had happened and had no idea about what was going to happen next. Finally, we were all lined up and we went inside. Mr Thompson asked us to sit on the floor.

"The first thing he said was that the very bad story Billy had told us that morning was made up. Yes, there had been a storm—everyone knew that. But no, there had not been a swaggie and there had not been a family and their dogs killed by anyone. All the outlying farms had been checked after the storm and, apart from some trees being blown over, there had been no serious damage to people, animals, or buildings.

"Mr Thompson told us that Fred had gone with Billy to the gaolhouse because Fred would go home and get their father. Mr Smith would have to go to the gaolhouse to get Billy and take him home. Then Mr Smith would have to come back to the school in the afternoon and talk to Mr Thompson about what Billy had said. Mr Thompson then thanked us for being so polite when the sergeant was there and told us we had all behaved very well after such an unhappy start to the morning. He said that he had some treats for us and that he had been going to give them to us after school, but he wanted to give them to us now because he appreciated the way we'd all behaved.

"And then he took a big bag of boiled sweets from the drawer in his desk and passed it around saying we could have one each. That had never happened at school before.

We thought it was just wonderful. And we thought Mr Thompson was wonderful, too. And he was such a good man. He was so thoughtful. He said that it wasn't fair for Fred to miss out because he had to do an unpleasant job for the sergeant and then he said that even though Billy had done the wrong thing, he would still get a sweet, too. He said he thought Billy would get enough punishment and so when he came back to school his sweet would be waiting for him.

"And I can't remember any other scary stories being told at school after that. It took a while, but the kids and their parents eventually began to smile when they talked about the 'swaggie story' and then it sort of became folklore. I don't think Billy Smith was ever a hero in anyone's eyes, but it amused me when some years later he and Juney Cooper got married.

"You're a good girl, Laura," she'd then say and give me a hug. "You always listen to my stories. You don't mind me telling them over and over. And so that's why today I want to tell you about this spot of mine, this place, here on the riverbank. It's not mine, not really. It's not anyone's. But it's always been special to me. Not just because I used to play here with my brothers and sisters, cousins and friends, but because it means so much more to me than that. Whenever my mother had a moment to herself, she always came here to this place. She couldn't explain it, either. I asked her a couple of times, and then again just before she died. She'd just say it felt like the right place for her. And it's been like that for me. It feels like the right place. And I think it might be a little bit like that for you too, Laura. You always look peaceful when you come here. And that's important to me. I know how busy you are, and I know you love being busy. But everyone needs a place to be peaceful and this, for whatever reason, is our place.

"So, we all know I'm not getting any younger." She smiled at me as she said this. "Don't interrupt me, Laura; you might think you know what I'm going to say, but I want you to hear my words. I am not sick. I am not dying. Not yet, anyway. And no, not anytime soon." She hugged me again.

"When that time comes, when it does happen, it's my wish that you take charge of the arrangements. There's an envelope with James, my solicitor, and there's another one for you. My wishes and my will are inside those envelopes. There's also an outline of my funeral service. Everyone knows I don't want a fuss. So, it'll be brief. And then, after everyone's said goodbye to me and comforted each other, I'll be cremated. And then, when you're ready, you'll gather the family together and scatter my ashes here. But before then, you'll arrange for a bench to be put here. It's not to be flash. I just want a bench for you and anyone else to come and sit and be peaceful. You can think of me if you want. I won't be hanging around to haunt you. I'll be back in the environment, the earth, the river, the air. And this will be your place.

"Oh, darling girl, cry if you have to. It's not going to happen for years. But this is what I want to have happen, here, in this place. Okay?"

I nodded and tried to smile at her.

And now, so many years later, as I sit on Nanna's log bench and look around this place, our place, I feel the longed-for peace settle around me. I often think of how I surprised Nanna by organising this bench in her place just for her, long before she passed away. In most of my earliest memories of coming here with her, we just sat on the ground. Sometimes she'd bring a picnic rug for us to sit on, usually after rain.

As she got older, Nanna would bring fold-up chairs for us. We'd put them in the back of the farm ute and park as close to her spot as we could. This went on for years. We'd often bring a basket with the thermos, mugs, teabags, and whatever biscuits she'd baked that week, and we'd enjoy morning or afternoon tea, relaxing, talking, and gossiping, but mostly just watching the river and its birdlife. I always made sure I was home for the annual backyard bird count.

Nanna and I and any other family members who could be there would always come to the riverbank and count the variety and number of birds we'd see in two or three hours. Nanna also counted the birds that came into the farm garden in the afternoon and early evenings. Over the years, she built up an incredible catalogue for both places.

Sometimes when we'd go to the riverbank, she'd bring her fishing rod and a few garden worms, or we'd grab a spool of dark cotton and a small piece of raw meat and catch yabbies. If she caught a fish, a real fish—not a "stinking carp", as she called them—she'd take it home and cook it. If we caught any yabbies, and mostly we did, we'd stockpile them for a little while and then gently pop them back in the water.

After her talk about wanting a bench here for the family for when we'd gather to scatter her ashes, I decided that she should have the benefit of the bench, too. Mum, Dad, and I talked about the best way to do this. We wanted something meaningful. Something more than just buying a bench from the local hardware store or garden centre, even though Nanna would have been happy with that.

Then Dad had a brainwave. He piled us into the farm ute and drove us just a little bit further along the riverbank. As long as he could remember, there'd always been a dead tree that had fallen over and was just resting on the riverbank.

He told us that, every now and then, he'd sit on that log and watch the river, the birds, the sky, the weather. He liked the idea of moving it to Nanna's special place, but he also liked the idea of getting one of the old timber cutters to shape it into a seat with a backrest for her.

Smiling and relaxing, I remember some of the other things that happened here: the talks with Nanna. Fishing and yabbying with her and also with Dad. Picnics and swimming with family and friends. Skinny-dipping with my girlfriends. And then, when we were older and thought we were so very sophisticated, drinking, smoking, and skinny-dipping with boys.

My special times of reading novels, studying, and writing some sad and bad poetry here with a thermos or an icy drink or—when I was older and felt truly sophisticated—with cheap wine, cheese, and biscuits. And the time, just after I'd graduated from high school and been accepted into university, coming here late at night with Shane. How high my expectations, my dreams, were that night. Shane Johnstone and me. Here. Me with stars in my eyes, passion in my heart, and violins in my mind, and Shane Johnstone, vice-captain of the football team. Year 12 heart-throb, tall, blonde and good-looking. Obviously, I'd read far too many romantic novels in the lead-up to this monumental event. The scratchy blanket on the ground that didn't soften the dead grass or the occasional sharp stone was nothing at all like sinking into the romantic king-sized bed I'd seen in the movies. There was no glowing scented candlelight or soft romantic music surrounding our passion. Looking back, I don't think there was much real passion, either. We fumbled and groped our way through my first time of "doing it" and—I realised later—defiling this very special place. Nanna would have been horrified.

Poor Shane. Poor me. Not much later, when he took me home, I was basically dropped off at the garden gate with what was probably a very embarrassed "See you, Laura. That was good. We'll catch up sometime, hey?" and then he was gone with the taillights shining through the darkness. What a relief. He was gone. And I wouldn't have to see him again. And I couldn't wait to get into the shower and wash myself clean. I still feel thankful that I'd been home alone. Mum, Dad, and Nanna had gone to a cattle sale and were away overnight. Yes, I had been a sneaky teenager, taking advantage of their absence. In some way, I'd also taken advantage of Shane, too.

Young love? Young passion? Young hormones, more likely. I can smile at the memory now as I feel the peace of this place surround me. Shane is now one of the local councillors. He's also the local chemist. He and Julie have four children and we're all good friends. I don't know if he's ever discussed that night with Julie and I don't want to know. It happened many years before they met.

This afternoon, as I feel myself surrounded by the peace of this place, I think of the talk Dad and I had this morning with his doctor. We cried. His words were almost an echo of those long-ago words of his mother, Nanna. And when the time comes, once more my family will gather at this special place and scatter his ashes. Once more, he will be with his mother and back together with Mum.

And, as if from some weird ritual from my younger days spent here in this place, I reach into the little old cane basket and take out a spool of black cotton, bite off a good length of it and tie a piece of raw meat to one end and lightly drop it into the water just out from the riverbank. Yabbying has been one of my most favourite things to do in this special place. When I'm not reminiscing.

Saturday

Hannah excitedly lifted the large box from the post office counter. "Thanks for this, Col," she said to the elderly man behind the counter with a smile. "Have a great afternoon, and good luck for the bowls competition tomorrow; I reckon you'll win again this year, and that'd be the trifecta before you retire to the coast. I'll cross my fingers, but you won't need it." She smiled at the people in the short queue behind her as she moved towards the doorway. Carrying the weighty box out to her dark blue hatchback, she fumbled with the keys in her pocket before managing to press the button and unlock it.

"Hey, Hannah," a voice called, "let me help; that looks heavy."

"Thanks, Jacko," she replied, looking up at the high school's tall Phys Ed teacher. "That'd be great. You'll be interested in this, I think," Hannah said with a grunt as she pushed the box into back of the car after he'd lifted up the hatchback's door for her. "It's the inflatable kayak I mentioned at morning tea on Wednesday." She grinned knowing she had his full attention.

"Yeah? Are you taking it out tomorrow? Suse and I'd love to come along. You know we head out around seven—is that too early for you? We could meet you down at the boat ramp and I'll give you a hand to blow it up? I reckon there'll be a hand or foot pump in the box," he continued enthusiastically, "but we've got a portable electric pump that only takes a couple of minutes. Can't wait to tell Suse. She'd love to have you come out with us."

"Sounds good to me, Jacko. I've been wanting to catch up with both of you. I'm thinking about lessons and a bit of training and wondered if Suse would take me on for some private lessons. With work and all that, I can only fit in the weekend mornings until the holidays. Can you mention that to her? Let her know it's not a problem if she can't fit me in, because I'm happy to wait, it's just that I'm keen to get started and want to learn properly; that way I shouldn't get it wrong or develop any bad habits."

"No worries, Han. I'll get her to ring you tonight and you can chat about it. You sound a bit serious; you're not just going to get out on the river and splash around for fun?""Oh, yeah, that'll probably be part of it, Jacko. But I've got a goal down the track a bit, so it's important to me that I get it right from the start."

"Yeah? Want to talk about it, or—" Jacko paused and looked at Hannah thoughtfully. "—is it one of those plans that people keep to themselves until they're ready to put it all into action?" He smiled, thinking that he knew what Hannah would say.

"Oh, I'm happy to talk to you and Suse about it, Jacko," she replied. "Of all the teachers and staff at school, I know you can keep things to yourself. I'm planning to paddle a length of the Murray this year and looking at doing the Massive Murray Paddle next year." She grinned at him again, knowing that he and Suse would be almost as excited about this as she was.

"Wow, Hannah. You're not mucking around, are you?" He grinned back at her. "I can't wait to tell Suse, and you know she won't be saying anything, either. Well, gotta go; see you bright and early at the boat ramp. You'll hang around for coffee and breakfast after, right? You can tell us all about it then. See you bright and early." She could hear him whistling one of his favourite country songs as his long legs strode along the street towards home and Suse to share the news.

Hannah opened the box as soon as she put it on her lounge room floor. Placing the manual and instructions to one side, she couldn't stop smiling as she took out the different items, carefully looking over each one.

This is easy, she thought, joining the paddle ends together and tightening the handle. While she couldn't wait to sit in the kayak, she decided to leave that until she saw Jacko and Suse in the morning. *If their pump works as well as he reckons,* she thought, *I'll get one of those, too.* Putting all the plastic and packaging back in the box, she carried it into the laundry. *Won't chuck it out just yet,* she thought. *Might need to use it if something's wrong with the thing, although it all looks pretty good to me.* Hannah realised she'd hardly stopped smiling since she left the post office.

After a quick chicken-and-salad dinner, Hannah picked up the paddle and perched herself on a stool. *Just a quick row,* she thought. *Surely, I can't get this wrong.* Then, after putting the paddle on the floor went over to the table for her phone. *Yep, there they are,* she thought happily, and she chose one of the online tutorials she'd located about kayaking for beginners.

Hannah had just finished watching the first one, feeling quite surprised about all the details and techniques outlined in the video. *Well, who would have guessed all that,* she thought. *So, you don't just get in, sit down, and paddle like mad.* As she scrolled through the list of tutorials, the buzzing vibration of an incoming text message startled her.

Who'll that be? she wondered, and then she smiled as Jacko's name glowed on her screen.

Hi Han, she read, here's a list of tutorials that Suse thought you might like to check out before we see you tomorrow. I forgot she has classes tonight and won't be home until later. The message with its links was followed by a couple of smiley faces.

Gr8 thks, she replied. Just watched one and it's the top on ur list. She added two smiley faces before C U 2morrow.

Deciding not to practise on the stool, Hannah showered before putting what she'd need into her backpack and placing it on the floor next to the kayak. Stretching and yawning, she reached out for her book before climbing into bed. When she'd read a couple of chapters, Hannah turned the reading light off and clicked on the radio, making sure she'd also hit its snooze button.

Birdsong and early morning sunshine woke her, and she eagerly rolled over and put her feet on the floor. Bathers, shorts, T-shirt, cap, sunscreen—Hannah mentally ticked the items off as she dressed and went into the kitchen to juice a couple of oranges before leaving. Fresh juice was one of her favourite morning routines and she rarely missed this part of her day. Knowing her full water bottle was sitting in the backpack's side pocket meant she was out the door and putting the kayak into the hatchback in readiness for its first outing sooner than she'd expected. Hannah raced back inside, this time grabbing the paddle and her backpack, and then she was in the car and backing onto the roadway.

She waved at Fred next door, who'd come out to get the morning paper off the lawn before his dog started chewing on it, and drove carefully along the quiet street, knowing that early morning joggers and cyclists would not be expecting to see cars at this time.

Hannah pulled into the car park at the boat ramp right behind Jacko and Suse. They waved at her before getting their kayaks off the roof rack. Suse put their pump on the ground near Hannah's car and waited for her new kayak to go next to it before hugging her.

"This is so exciting, Han," she said. "We can't wait to see you get out there and give you a hand with your training. Have you been thinking about this for a while? It's not a spur of the moment thing, is it, because sometimes they just don't work out that well. Not that I want to be negative, but the number of people who've come along for one or two lessons and then store their kayak or sell it because it didn't suit them is amazing for such a small town. I think some of them have a go when they're on holidays at the coast and think they'll keep it up, but that rarely happens." Suse looked at her closely, "No," she said thoughtfully, "you'd have put a fair bit of thought and research into this I reckon." She cocked her head as she waited for Hannah's response.

Hannah grinned, thinking she could say anything and Suse would probably believe her but went with the facts.

"Yeah, I've done some research, Suse, and I have been thinking about it for a while. I just wanted the mornings and the water to get warmer before I started doing anything. I've got a cousin who lives in Echuca, and we've decided that we're going to paddle down the Murray from Picnic Point to Moama Beach before Christmas, before the river gets too busy with tourists, so I need to know I can manage a four- or six-hour paddle. Even though we don't know how long it'll take us to do that stretch of the river, I'd rather be over-prepared and do it easy than struggle. What do you think?"

"I don't think you're mucking around with this, Hannah," she replied. "It sounds like fun, and moving with the river will be much easier than going upstream. It probably won't be too easy, but I reckon you'll be right. And you've thought about it a fair bit, so that's good, too. Rightio, Jacko, here's Hannah's kayak. You get her started with the pump while I go and grab the sunscreen. You'll find the portable electric pump so much easier and faster than a foot or hand pump, Han," Suse called out as she moved across to their car.

Hannah carefully watched Jacko connect the pump to her kayak and was pleased to see it fully inflated in just a couple of minutes. After locking the pump back in his car, Jacko joined them as they carried the kayaks down the boat ramp and into the warm shallow water.

"If you watched those training videos last night, you should be right getting in, Hannah," Suse called, "but I just want to let you know that I fell out twice the first time I tried kayaking, and all that happens is you get wet." She laughed as she paddled out into deeper water.

"Oh, and embarrassed," she continued. "I thought everyone was watching me and laughing at me, but they weren't. Everyone I know's fallen out at least once; it's almost a rite of passage. Wow! Look at you go—you're a natural!" Suse clapped as Hannah shot her a big grin before slowly paddling out to join her.

"Okay, girls," Jacko called. "I'm heading upstream and will see you in about half an hour or so, depending where you decide to go. Have fun, Han; see you later, Suse." He waved his paddle at them before turning his kayak and taking off, heading up towards the bridge.

"I thought you might like to practise turning and starting and stopping, Han," Suse said. "It looks like you've got a good grip on the handle and it's in the right position, so we'll do a couple of drills and then set off upstream. That'll make it easier coming back if your muscles start feeling it. You're pretty fit, but this is a new workout for some of your muscles, and if they don't let you know now, they certainly will later on.

"We'll do some basic stretching when we've finished, and if you've got time this arvo, you might like to do a few laps in the pool. That'll help with the stretching and keep your arm and shoulder muscles nice and warm. If you'd like to come out again tomorrow morning, let me know. I haven't got any classes tomorrow, but I would like to give you a follow-up before next weekend and I know how busy you guys are when the kids go home. The days just aren't long enough yet to have a couple of afternoons out on the water when you've finished school for the day.

"And, while I think of it, if you liked the way the pump worked this morning, I saw they're on special down at the auto place. It'll save you time and help keep your enthusiasm up, although from what I can see and from what Jacko said, you're pretty motivated. Tell me about that first bit of the Murray you're doing with your cousin in the holidays."

Hannah spoke cautiously as she concentrated on paddling, and then suddenly, she felt as if everything clicked into place, and she looked up to see Suse grinning at her. "Yep, you've got it, girl! Everything's in rhythm, your stroke's good, your upper body turning's good and you're in control. Just stay focused on the actions, but look up and around and enjoy the view and keep on talking. I'm loving what I'm hearing."

Twenty minutes later, they'd moved through the main part of town, past the golf course and tennis club, and Hannah had seen her town from a new vantage point for the first time.

"Oh, Suse, this is fantastic. I have no idea why I haven't done this sooner. The town looks great from here and seeing the ducks and water birds and the houses with their gardens coming down to the walking path. It's all so lovely. Yep, I'll be back tomorrow morning for more of this." She smiled as Suse indicated they should stop paddling and just drift for a while.

"It is great, isn't it, Han?" she replied. "And you've just reinforced something Jacko and I've been talking about for a while now. The river's not getting half the use and enjoyment it should. We know it's not big or wide enough for skiing and there's the always lake for the skiers. We're thinking about applying to council to set up kayak rentals over summer. The public liability's the big hurdle, but we reckon, once people see just how nice it is out here, then hourly rentals for locals and visitors should make it all viable. And we've considered group tours and small group lessons as well as one-on-one coaching. We talked about this again last night and wanted to see how you went today, but if this goes ahead, would you be interested in taking guided kayak tours every now and then over the holidays if you're not going away? You've proved to me that you're capable, so it'd just be doing a few more hours, and you've already got your first aid and CPR certificates for work, so you'd just need your lifesaving certificate. What d'ya think? Oh, look, here's Jacko now." Suse waved enthusiastically at her husband as he paddled over to them.

The three of them paddled companiably back to the boat ramp, chatting about their plans and how Hannah could be included if she wanted.

"You know, Suse," Hannah said, "it's a great idea, a great plan, and I think I'd love to be part of it, but first, I need to do the Murray paddle with my cousin. Now I've had a taste, I'm really keen to do that. And," she continued thoughtfully, "doing that first stretch with Rob would give me more credibility as a guide, wouldn't it?"

Jacko nodded as he grinned at Suse and Hannah. "It sure would. Hey, Suse—let's get these stacked and yours deflated and get breakfast. We'll talk more then. C'mon, girls, let's go." Hannah dried her kayak with a chamois cloth as she rolled it up, giving it a little pat and whispering to it how well it had behaved for her and how much she'd enjoyed the morning's paddle. Looking around to make sure she had all her gear, she waved to Jacko and Suse before driving off to the Take-a-Break café.

Enjoying their breakfast and coffee and chatting about work and local community events while greeting and acknowledging locals and past and present students, time flew.

Suse grabbed her last piece of toast and stood, reminding them that her first kayak class would soon start. Jacko stood to leave with her, and Hannah smiled at them, realising just what a great couple they made.

Hannah insisted on shouting breakfast as Suse had been happy to guide her through the first session and then told her that just going out on the river together would be all the lessons or instruction that Han would need.

"Just check on what the lifesaving certificate needs, Han," Suse reminded her as she moved away from their table. "You could probably do it here at the pool or, if not, in one of the bigger towns along the highway. Check it out and let me know. See you tomorrow morning." They left her to finish her coffee and reflect on her progress as a new kayaker. Grinning, Hannah reached for her phone and sent a photo and text to her cousin, proving that she'd started her training and asking if he'd made a start on his.

We've got just on eight weeks left before I come knocking on your door, she texted, so you make sure you're fit and ready to go. Adding a smiley face, she hit send.

Hannah rolled her shoulders as she walked back to her car. *Right,* she thought, *a swim with a few laps this afternoon, but before then I'm going to see if I can get a massage.* She located the number and was able to book an upper back massage for just after lunchtime. Next, she called into the auto shop and bought an electric pump like the one Jacko had used.

Heading back home, Hannah was able to get through her weekend housework and a bit of gardening before having a quick shower and leaving for her much-anticipated massage.

Later on, as she stretched out on the couch, Hannah sipped her glass of wine and reflected on her busy day. *And there's more to come tomorrow,* she thought happily. Reaching out for her phone, Hannah quickly sent a text to Suse, thanking her for a great time out on the river and saying that she'd see her same time, same place in the morning.

And that's my Saturday, she mused, *done and dusted.*

Spotlighting

Jackson stopped his ute in a scatter of dust outside the house fence instead of parking it in the shed as usual. Almost as soon as he'd turned the ignition off, he was out the door and running through the gate. The sun had just dropped below the horizon and the soft evening twilight was not yet full of shadows.

"Dad, Dad!" he yelled as he jumped up onto the veranda. "There's a couple of foxes in the front paddock, and some of those ewes are likely to drop their lambs tonight." He quickly kicked his work boots off and raced through the screen door, letting it slam behind him.

"Dad," he called again. "I'm gonna ring Shane and James and see if they're able to come spotlighting tonight. D'ya want to give Uncle Matt a ring? He might like to come, or we can go through his paddocks too if he'd like. I'm ringing Shane now," he continued as he pushed the keys on his phone. "I'll need the gun and some ammo; can you get the key for the gun safe for me?"

"Whoa, slow down, son," came his father's softly spoken reply. "Where were they—near the road or back towards the fence? Not that it matters, of course—they'll be moving—but we'd better get the word out. These'd be the first that you've spotted this lambing season, wouldn't they?"

Jackson nodded as he heard the phone ringing at the other end. "Hey, Shane—foxes in our front paddock; two of the bastards. I'll be spotlighting tonight; wanna come? Good; see you soon, then. I'm about to ring James, and I think Dad'll ring Uncle Matt."

He looked up and grinned at his father. "Yep, the boys'll come. Have you been able to get in touch with Uncle Matt?" He then focused his attention on the phone in his hand as he heard it ringing on James's number.

"Mate." Jackson spoke quickly. "Foxes at our place. Shane's coming, can you? Dad's ringing Uncle Matt? Great. See you soon."

"Yep, Dad, they'll be here soon. What's Uncle Matt saying?" He paused to listen to his favourite uncle's voice coming through his father's phone.

Father and son smiled at each other. "Well, Jackson, we'll all be spotlighting tonight by the sound of things." Phil smiled as he looked at the tall young man in front of him. "Those bloody foxes sure are going to be sorry they let you see them. Good timing on your part, though. I heard Harry Cooper had a bit of trouble at his place last night. Foxes got a couple of newborns. He'd been out around the paddocks a couple of times, too. They're sneaky bastards, that's for sure. If we can get the two you saw and any others tonight, that'll be a good night's spotlighting.

"Mum's not home yet, so make a couple of sandwiches, will you? There's ham and cheese in the fridge. Make enough for the five of us; we can eat as we drive. I'll get the guns and ammo out of the safe and we'll be ready to go when Matt and the boys get here. I reckon we could easy put in two or three hours tonight. We'll check the sheep as well as keep our eyes open for those bloody mongrels."

Phil rubbed his hands together in anticipation. "There's nothing like the thought of a good night's spotlighting to get your energy going after a full day's work," he said to his son. "And it's a nice-looking night out there, too: half-moon, so it won't be too bright. Is the spotty still up on your ute?" Jackson nodded as he buttered the bread for the sandwiches.

"Good. Whatever we get tonight, you and the boys can have the bounty if you want to take them into the DPI."

"Yeah, thanks, Dad. We'll see, though. I've always liked hanging them on the fence for a day or two, it's just the stink when you go to take the tails. That always gets to me. And I still haven't worked out whether or not hanging them up like that scares other foxes off. Sometimes I think it does, other times I think it's a load of crap from old blokes. What d'ya reckon, Dad? You've never really said."

"Well, mate, that's because I just don't know. I'm of the same mind as you. I know years ago we always used to hang the mongrels up, and then we'd go out night after night for a week or two and not see any. But that didn't mean they weren't there; they might have just gone to ground. Then, when the bounty went to ten dollars a tail, that paid for the ammo after a good night's shooting, so we'd either chuck the carcases in a hole and cover it with a bit of dirt or throw them onto a pile of logs and burn 'em. They stink enough when they're roadkill, you don't want a night's shooting just lying around dead in your paddocks.

"Here's someone now; sounds like Matt's ute. I'll go and get the door. Looks like you've just about finished there. Hey, Matty, how's things?" Phil asked his youngest brother and neighbour, who was kicking off his workbooks before stepping inside.

"Great, thanks, Phil. Hey, Jackson. How are you both? Kimberley not home from work yet?"

Phil shook his head. "No, she had a couple of clients booked in for after work, so she'll be a while yet. I've sent her a text so she won't be interrupted by the phone. Ah!" He checked his phone when it buzzed. "She's replied: *Go get 'em, boys*. Sure will," he said as he sent a thumbs up to his wife.

At the sound of two vehicles pulling up near the fence, the men all went outside. Phil and Jackson made sure their guns' safety catches were on and that they pointed towards the ground before walking out to the vehicles.

"Boys." Phil nodded to Shane and James, long-time family friends and good mates with Jackson. "Looks like there's going to be a bit of action in the paddocks tonight, if we're lucky and the foxes aren't. Jackson's ute's ready to go; if you'd like to get in the back, Phil and I'll go in his. Straight shooting, boys, and be careful," he said as he climbed into Phil's passenger seat. "Jackson's made some sandwiches, so make sure you eat them before the action kicks off; we'll all concentrate better with a bit of fuel in us. Right, meet you down at the gate." He gave a quick wave as Phil started his ute and turned around to drive back along the farm track.

"Thanks, Jackson, looks good," Shane said as he bit into his sandwich. "Do you want to drive, or I could so you can get a few shots in."

"Sounds good to me, mate," Jackson replied, vaulting up into the back of his ute. "Let's get going. How've you been, James? Did you get that fencing job finished?"

The young men talked as they stood in the ute's tray, occasionally leaning down to speak to Shane through the open windows. Shane stopped next to Phil's vehicle at the open gate leading into the farm's front paddock. They all looked around and waved as a neighbour drove his tractor past. Unsurprisingly, Wayne indicated and turned into the farm entrance, stopped his tractor and walked over to them. "Bit of spotlighting tonight, hey?" he asked with a big grin. "Have you seen any, or are you just having a look around?"

"Wayne," Phil replied, "Jackson spotted two on his way home before. Hopefully we'll get them and any more that might be around. Harry Cooper lost a couple of newborns overnight, so we're going into his paddocks, too. In a hurry, or would you like to come along?"

"I'll just text Marg and let her know and I'll join in. Gun's not with me, but that doesn't matter; I'll be another pair of eyes for you." He grinned as he hit the send button. "She'll reply when she can, but she won't mind me getting home a bit later than I said; she hates bloody foxes as much as the rest of us. Never forgiven the mongrels after they got in the chook pen that time." He shook his head at the memory of their slaughtered hens.

"Rightio, here's the plan. Shane, you take Jackson's ute along the road fence; we'll go up along this one. Make sure you stop and unload the guns before we get back close to each other. Keep your eyes open and shoot straight. Check out the sheep as well; see if any have dropped their lambs and take a look in case they need a hand. They should all be right, though; they're a healthy lot this year. We'll meet back here in half an hour or so and then head over into the next paddock. Then we'll move into Harry's paddock. I've let him know the outline of what we're doing, so he'll be expecting us in an hour or so. Good luck; let's go."

As twilight deepened into the darkness of night, both utes slowly drove through the paddocks, their spotlights shining an arc through the dying light. Jackson carefully worked the spotty, knowing that James was also looking well beyond its glow, searching for the giveaway yellow eyes that might stop and look back at them. Knowing this was a slow process that drivers, spotters, and shooters all needed to concentrate on, kept their voices soft and engines as quiet as possible.

Jackson flinched automatically when a shot rang out. Even though he'd hoped to hear the sound of a gun, the noise was startling as it cracked through the quietness. He grinned at James, knowing they both hoped they'd get a turn soon. Before long, however, they'd completed their circuit, stopping only to check on a sheep and its newborn lamb. It was no secret that Shane loved lambs, and he quickly jumped out of the cab to check the baby animal and take a photo before patting it and moving away before he upset its mother.

Not much later, both utes met at the paddock gate. "We got one," Phil said. "I think there might have been another one. I was focused on this one, and Wayne got a clear shot at it. Dropped it on the spot. Matty said he'd seen another one just off to its right, but it'd gone as soon as Wayne fired. We looked around for a while, but once they're gone, that's it. They don't hang around. Well, no luck for you yet?" He looked at his son.

"Nope, but Shane got to pat a new baby," Jackson said with a smile. "That's made his night."

No-one laughed; a love of animals was something they all knew and respected, and the privilege of taking care of them and the enjoyment that a safe birth gave was part of farming life.

"Okay, then," Phil replied. "Let's head into the next paddock. Shane, you go along up that line, and we'll do the road fence. Meet you back here in about thirty minutes or so. Keep your eyes open and the guns safe. See you soon." The little party of shooters headed back into the darkness with only headlights and spotties to light the way across the paddocks.

By the time the moon had dropped low in the sky, six foxes had met their death. The men were pleased with their night's work, knowing that, for now, mobs of sheep on two farms were safer and more protected than they had been just a few hours earlier. Aching backs from standing in ute trays as they bounced across paddocks and sore arm muscles from holding guns and working spotlights were of no consequence.

A good night's spotlighting was over, and a hot cuppa with a good yarn was the next thing on the list.

The Show

While detailed planning and hard work had been going on for months, now community anticipation was building. As soon as the district's annual show schedule had been published and trekked around to local businesses for people to collect when convenient, numerous individual projects had begun, some well in advance. And many of those projects were dependent on the weather.

Spring is an uncertain season in this little part of the country. Some years, it brings unheralded heat, flies, and vicious thunderstorms. Other years are a continuation of the dry winter, often heralding an unwanted and dreaded period of drought. Occasionally, winter would casually scatter one last chilly stretch of frost to eventually melt away once the pale sunlight slowly caressed the air and earth. This year, spring's smile was far too brief. Plants and gardens, confused by sudden and extreme changes in temperature, became sullen and uncooperative despite the careful attention of tireless, hardworking gardeners.

On the day before entries across all sections of the show closed, the chief steward (horticulture) stepped out from her pavilion and took stock of the cloudless blue sky stretching from one horizon to the other. Today, the midmorning sun beamed brilliantly over the showgrounds, highlighting the irrigators splashing precious drops of water on soft green grass in the show ring. She watched the relentless dust cast by vehicles delivering goods throughout the showgrounds hover above and around the showring, mocking the glistening water droplets even as they fell onto the thirsty ground.

"And it's not yet summer," she murmured as her mouth twisted wryly from its usual cheery smile to something more pensive and patient. Lifting her hand in a quick wave, she acknowledged one of the younger men driving a ute stocked with various farm produce to the agricultural pavilion before turning back into the welcoming coolness behind her.

Meanwhile, gardeners of all ages and abilities kept working, watering and weeding their beloved plants, garden beds, and flower tubs, coaxing, cajoling, and sometimes lightly threatening the growth and colour that they caressed and carefully tended before apprehensively delivering them to the horticulture pavilion for cataloguing, classifying, judging, and public display.

For months, just like the gardeners, many competitive and dedicated cooks had been determinedly whisking, beating, stirring, and practising their favourite recipes, sometimes experimenting with new ones for previously unentered classes in the cookery section. Likewise, unintimidated weekend or casual cooks shook off the mental cobwebs that had gathered since the previous show, flexed their enthusiasm, and then dived headfirst into pots, pans, mixing bowls, and freshly bought ingredients.

This whirlwind of baking, preserving, creating, and decorating rippled out across the town and countryside as results were tasted and shared or sometimes fed to surprised but happy dogs and chooks before the whole process began again.

Late in the evening before show day, and after entering her efforts and chatting to stewards and other hopeful cooks, one young weekend cook wandered from the cookery pavilion to the agriculture shed and its displays. A farmer's daughter, she'd spent much of her life involved with carting hay, stacking hay bales, and then feeding it to their cattle. Delightedly, she'd hand-fed it to her favourite animals. For years, she'd seen the hay grow, helped irrigate it, and watched as it was mown and baled. She'd breathed its rich luxuriant fragrance and brushed wisps of it from her hair, socks, boots, and clothing before entering the house. She'd rubbed it lightly from tired, dry eyes after long days of work and late nights of helping get it off the paddocks before the storms came. These thoughts passed through her mind as she wandered wearily along the row of stacked hay bales waiting to be judged.

Suddenly she froze, taking in the quality of those in front of her. Carefully, casually, she turned, retracing her steps to the cookery pavilion. Once out of sight, she hurried through the encroaching darkness back to the cattle sheds. "Where's Frank?" she asked a fellow farmer. "Have you seen him in the last ten or fifteen minutes? He hasn't gone over to the tin shed yet, has he?"

"No, mate," came the laconic reply as he pointed to three figures standing at the end of the sheds. "He's down there talking to Sid and Len."

"Great. Thanks, Doug." She was off again, dragging a show program and pen from the depths of her shoulder bag.

"Hey, guys," she called, sauntering casually towards them. "How's things?" As she listened to their friendly replies, her eyes indicated to Frank that she wanted to speak to him. "Got a minute, Frank?" she asked. "Just need to ask you something."

Frank carefully masked his surprise as he nodded. "Sure Kate. I'll catch you later, Sid, Len." Nodding as he touched the brim of his Akubra, he walked off with her.

"What's up, love?" he asked his young neighbour. "You're going to think I'm nuts, Frank, but have you got a couple of spare bales of lucerne?" "You need some hay, love?"

"No, not me. I'd like you to fill out the entry form and take a couple of bales over to the ag pavilion. Trust me, you'll do well." Kate smiled at his confused expression. "Look, here, take this," she said, passing him a ten-dollar note. "I'm shouting your entry fee," she said with a grin. "Please, Frank, just do it. You've only got twenty minutes."

"Got a bet on this, have you, Katie?" He smiled down at her.

"God, no." She laughed back. "I've just come from there. Your hay's a winner. Quick, go." Laughing, she gave the man she'd known and respected all her life a light shove as she reached out to tuck her blue note into his shirt pocket. Grinning back at her and patting the pocket, Frank shook his head as he moved to complete the task he'd been set. After carefully loading five bales into the back of his ute, he slowly drove across the darkness of the showgrounds to the brightly lit agricultural shed. People were busily scurrying around with their farm produce before being directed to the relevant sections.

"G'day, Howard," Frank said, handing the chief steward Kate's money and the completed entry form. "Got some lucerne hay for you." Smiling, he walked back out to his ute to lift the bales out and carry them inside.

"Here, Mr Jackson, let me give you a hand." Frank turned and smiled in surprise.

"G'day, Lachie. Didn't expect to see you here tonight. Shouldn't you be at school?"

"No, sir. I finished Year 12 last year. I'm doing my gap year with Pa before uni next year."

"Uni, hey, Lachie? What are you going to study?" "Agronomy at UNE. It's not that far away and I reckon it's the way of the future. People have got to eat and the planet's getting more and more people every day."

"Well, you're not wrong there, Lachie. Don't know why I hadn't heard that's what you're doing. And what'll you do about cricket this year? Play at uni?"

"That, and most of the season here. Uni doesn't start until February and, if we make the finals, I'll come home those weekends. Gee, this sure is good hay, Mr Jackson," the young man said as he carried two bales into the pavilion."Thanks Lachie, Kate thought so too." he said with a grin. "She bullied me into bringing it over from the cattle sheds."

"Ha! That'd be Kate, alright. What's she up to these days? Seems like ages since I've seen her, too."

"Well, come back to the cattle yards with me. We'll get her and a few of the others and go for a beer, what d'ya reckon?"

"Sounds good. I'd like that, sir."

"Bugger that 'sir' business, Lachie," Frank said as he slapped the young man on his shoulder. "I think it's about time you started calling me Frank."

Lachie's face lit up. "Dad always said—" For a moment, the light went out of his eyes and the happiness left his face. He swallowed. "Dad always said when the men of the district told kids to use their first name, they thought of them as grown up." He blinked tears away.

Frank swallowed and blinked too. "And he was right. Your dad was one of the best, and losing him in that bloody car accident in that storm was a real tragedy. I reckon he'd be proud of you, Lachie. Now, let's get those people and go get that coldie. You're swagging it here tonight, aren't you? Not driving home?"

"No, sir … Frank," he said with a smile. "I told Pa I'd help out and stay the night. It's always a bit of fun and a good way to catch up with people I haven't seen for a while. Show days are always so busy, with so much going on. I've offered to help Howard around the ag shed over the weekend, so a quiet beer tonight will be good. It's been a busy few days getting things ready."

Well before nine o'clock the next morning, everything was done and in place. The show ground's main gates opened to a small crowd of exhibitors eager to see how their work had been judged. While each one admitted to eagerness, almost all of them accepted the reality that theirs might not have been judged the best. This was what it meant to take part. They all knew that—whether or not their work received a small piece of blue, red, or yellow marked cardboard—they were an important part of the show. They also knew that some of the onlookers, those who stood and admired and compared the flowers, the cakes, the conserves, and the art and craft work, almost envied the courage and confidence it took to take part. To 'have a go'.

And, many of the exhibitors thought, when some of those onlookers saw a plate of scones that hadn't risen evenly or weren't evenly coloured, or a cake with a definite dip in its middle, or flowers that were already wilting and past their best, this could be the catalyst for them to 'have a go' and be part of the next show. Every exhibitor could all think back to the moment when they'd decided that this would be the year they'd enter something, and each one knew just what it took to follow through on that decision.

And so, all across the showgrounds, exhibitors, competitors and their families and friends spoke to interested onlookers of all ages, answering questions, encouraging conversations, explaining the work behind the exhibits and, when and where possible, supporting their interest and offering encouragement for their participation in the next show. Only the truly interested and dedicated would persevere, they knew.

Meanwhile, the president and a few show society committee members welcomed their official guests, including local and state politicians, show ambassadors, and representatives of other show societies. To many of them, this was one of those occasions where they'd visit each other's shows, network, learn, and mingle with established and new exhibitors across all sections and discuss entries and their quality with the stewards of each section.

While there were frequent bursts of laughter from the group as they moved around the showgrounds, nothing was taken lightly, and the underlying discussions were often quite serious. As most of the group were well known throughout the community, many people enjoyed the seeming incongruity of burly, weather-beaten farmers and graziers in serious conversation with the horticulture, cookery, and arts and crafts stewards, while those gathered around the pens of beef and stud cattle rings and the dog and poultry sheds smiled and welcomed the keen gardeners, cooks, and artists who visited their areas.

As the afternoon faded into evening and the tired riders and horses from the equestrian events left the showring arenas, the after-work crowds began streaming through the gates. Seats were reserved around the show ring, with blankets, coats, and cushions marking places while one or two family members stayed put and others went in search of food and drink.

The official party was escorted through crowded pavilions and sheds by chief stewards, and prize-winning exhibits were acknowledged and admired. In the agriculture shed, the president looked puzzled for a brief moment as he watched his lifelong friend Frank Jackson laughing with a group of farmers and young people as they discussed the champion lucerne hay entries. *There's a story there,* he thought as he caught snippets of the conversation. He'd never known Frank to enter his hay before and wondered why he had this year. *And it's not "beginner's luck", either,* he thought. Frank Jackson was well known across the district for the quality of his lucerne and had several lucrative feed contracts with horse breeding stables across the state. The president grinned over at Frank and, giving him the thumbs up, indicated they'd catch up later.

Early evening was the time the show's president really enjoyed touring sideshow alley with the official party. He knew most of the Showman's Guild members by name, if not by sight. Nodding, waving, and stopping to chat with some of the older ones also allowed him to estimate the numbers of young families and teens who were ready for the fun and excitement of the rides. Young parents with toddlers and babes in arms lined up for the brightly coloured teacup ride, those with older kids were in line at the dodgem cars, while some parents whose kids had convinced them they were old enough to drive themselves, waited and watched as the cars bounced and bumped through the chaos and noise.

The president smiled as he overheard some possibly bored fathers discussing their thoughts on the economics of dodgem rides. *It might look like easy money,* he thought, *but it's not an easy life.* He waved and nodded as he called a greeting to Joe and Shane. *And I'm sure I've heard you two discussing the economics of smashed avo as well,* he thought good-naturedly.

Further on, the official party stood and watched as teenagers screamed and laughed their way through the Octopus, the Hurricane, and other anti-gravity torture rides before making their way through amusement games including the laughing clowns and dart or ball throwing contests to the relative sanity of the jumbo slide and various jumping castles.

Kids carrying showbags and smothering their faces in fairy floss streamed through the stalls and the crowd.

Patient parents loaded their arms with goodies as they agreed to "just one more ride, pleeease" from their littlies before explaining that they would soon be heading to the ringside seats for the night program. And every now and then, a balloon would break free and drift up and above the crowd while its former owner bellowed, cried, or laughed at the sight.

Still nodding and smiling at faces in the crowd, many of which he'd known all his life, he grinned when he saw some of the town's charming senior citizens who'd obviously left their impeccable table manners at home as they battled the challenges of sauce-coated dagwood dogs, the Rotary Club's generously filled hamburgers, or overflowing baked potatoes. *Ah, the show,* he thought happily. *It brings out the kid in all of us.* After completing the circuit of the showgrounds, the official party made their way to the front of the showring for the opening ceremony. The president had been involved in one capacity or another for so long now that he was pleased that the number of invited guests had been reduced and so, too, had their speeches. Like so many people seated around the ring, he was ready for the night program, the entertainment, and the highlight of the fireworks. He'd always loved fireworks. And this year, after cancellations caused by the global pandemic, the fireworks did not disappoint.

His memories of a previous night program master of ceremonies enthusing the crowd by calling out the highest-flying colours of red, blue, silver, or gold were just that: a long ago memory. These days—or nights—the fireworks and light drones were carefully choreographed to a mood-enhancing soundtrack that, decades ago, could never have been predicted.

Then he reached out to the chief steward (horticulture) and, gently taking his wife's hand, raised it to his lips and said softly, "It's been another great show, darling; thank you for all you've done. What do you reckon about next year? Happy to give it another go? Look"—he gestured at the crowd around the show ring—"Look at all those happy faces. We've been a part of making this happen; isn't it marvellous?"

And at that moment, as the smoke from the last fireworks drifted away up into the darkness and just before the floodlights came back on, he saw the face of the woman he'd loved and been married to for almost fifty years smile back at him and nod. "Yes, Bob; let's give it one more year," she softly replied.

The Visitor

Georgia flicked off her dark blue Audi's cruise control and began slowing to the designated speed limit on the outskirts of the small, regional town. *Almost there,* she thought and rolled her shoulders in anticipation of a much-needed stretch once out of the car.

As her car continued to slow, she noted the industrial area on both sides of the highway and signs pointing to the racecourse, the location of the cattle saleyards or livestock exchange, and another advising the current fire risk status.

She smiled at the town's huge *Welcome* sign and admired the colourful garden bed at its base, thinking that it was indeed a very welcome contrast from the rough dry grass lining the roadside for the last two hundred or so kilometres. As the industrial area gave way to shady tree-lined residential streets, Georgia noted the tidy green lawns between the mostly small, well-established homes and fences or footpaths.

Glancing around, her eyes located the tallest structures the town boasted: grain silos and the water tower. Focusing her eyes back onto the road, which she realised had now become a street, she determined that her car was just under the legal speed limit before cresting the bridge crossing the river and entering the main business district.

Three pubs; one for each night I'm here, she thought before noticing the brightly signed RSL club and a street sign advertising the sports tavern. *Spoilt for choice.* She grinned, knowing that she'd be asking her accommodation's receptionist for dining recommendations.

Slowly gliding along the main street, she saw a cheerful-looking coffee shop and its outdoor tables decorated with small vases of flowers before moving into the central intersection and its stop sign. Waiting for two elderly pedestrians to cross the roadway, Georgia admired the entrance to the historical primary school grounds opposite an attractive park where she could see the brightly coloured, almost obligatory exercise stations situated in clumps of shady trees beside the walking path.

Any remaining work tension left her as she slowly relaxed into the thought of five days' peace and quiet away from the city and the almost non-stop work on her latest court case. Yes, her slimy client had been granted bail, but Georgia knew it would be opposed.

By God, she thought, *I'd oppose it too, if I could.* Her green eyes darkened at the thought of having to defend this sleaze again. *Nope*, she thought. *No way. Stuff him. He'll get another lawyer, one who's not as rigid, uptight, and moralistic as me.* While she'd managed to keep smiling, her eyes had narrowed during his tirade of insults, and Georgia was proud of the way she hadn't let him see that they'd affected her.

"Thank you, Mister Blondestowe," she'd replied with just the slightest emphasis on the *Mister*. Despite his numerous requests, then instructions, Georgia had refused to address him by his first name, Harold. "You'll find our receptionist has your account ready for you. It will need to be paid in the next five minutes or there will be an additional charge for any part of the following half hour, with no discount applicable." She had turned and walked into her office with its views out over the city skyline, firmly closing the door behind her.

Georgia later apologised to Rebecca for abandoning her to the sleazy Mister Blondestowe and, together, they ensured that his cheque with its angry-looking writing would be honoured by his bank. After work, Georgia and Rebecca had quietly discussed the obnoxious man and general aspects of his case as they sat comfortably at the bar of a nearby inner-city hotel.

"Of course, the prosecutor will oppose bail," Georgia had said, lifting her glass of wine. She'd already indicated this to her partners. "There will be some small legality that they'll find under their microscope, but I won't be dealing with it. As of—" She looked at her diamond-encrusted watch. "—twenty minutes ago, I'm on leave. And that's what I'll be doing: leaving town." She smiled at Rebecca. "Where do exhausted lawyers go on leave, Bec?" she mused, hoping that Rebecca would take the bait.

"Bali's nice this time of year, Georgia, but why not spoil yourself and go somewhere fancy in Europe? You haven't had a decent break for what, twelve months? No, it's been much longer than that. Where would you like to go?"

"Hmm, there's a thought. I might do some browsing over the weekend. Have a good one, Bec. You were a darling dealing with that sleazebag this afternoon. I'm now going home to shower the residue away. Remember that I won't be in for the next five weeks. I'll let you know where I decide to go in case you need to contact me, but anyway, you've got my mobile number." And after a quick brush of cheeks, Georgia was out of the bar and gone. *Just like that,* she thought. *And now, here I am, in the last place anyone from the city would think to look.* A spot on the map in rural New

South Wales. A spot she'd chosen after scrolling through a Facebook page designed for "SOLO road trips"—single older ladies on road trips—Georgia had smiled at that. "Why would you have to be older to go on a road trip?" she murmured, looking at the photos of country views, pub meals, and enjoying the author's pithy comments about taking her book out to dinner.

Indicating once more, Georgia turned off the roadway and carefully drove into the Deluxe Artesian Spa Motel reception area and turned off the ignition. Opening the door and getting out of the air-conditioned comfort made her gasp. The hot dry air with hardly any breeze felt as overwhelming as a bear hug. Slowly making her way towards the office, Georgia grimaced as she moved. She'd been driving without a break for longer than the recommended two hours and her back and shoulders knew it. She paused, stretched, then rolled her aching shoulders and looked around the motel's facilities. Yes, indoor and outdoor pools and a gym. They would soon be put to good use, she decided.

Entering the cool refreshing air in the reception area, Georgia smiled at the two women behind the desk. Their formal greetings over, Georgia signed the forms she'd completed online the afternoon before and, taking the key card to her suite, asked about gym hours and local dining recommendations.

"Our restaurant is four stars," the older woman, Marie, informed her with a kind smile. "And if you stay longer in the gym or pool than you intended, we can provide room service. Depending on your appetite, you might just like to order an entrée and dessert with wine and coffee. Otherwise, the kitchen closes at eight. As it's a weeknight, we won't be overrun, so take your time if you'd like to eat with us."

"Thanks so much," Georgia replied. "I'll see how I feel. The heat really surprised me when I got out of the car. Thanks again." Smiling, she gave a slight wave as she turned and left.

Parking outside her queen-sized unit and carrying her luggage in was almost as much as she felt like doing until she opened the bar-fridge and found bottles of flavoured sparkling mineral water. Pouring some into a tall glass with ice cubes and a slice of lemon from the complimentary fruit bowl on the bench, she turned on the air conditioner—a nice quiet one, she gratefully realised—and then slowly took in her surroundings.

It was spacious—more spacious than she'd anticipated—with a relaxing décor that suited the way she felt. *Yes*, Georgia thought tiredly, *I am exhausted. I am ready to relax; in fact, I'm ready to stop.* She pulled herself up at the thought. Stop? Stop what? *Stop the rat-race* was her first response. *Well,* she mused, *I don't think I saw that coming. But right now, after that good, cold drink, I'm going for a swim.*

This time, Georgia was ready for the heat that lurked mercilessly outside her now-cool suite. Without pausing, she moved over to the pool complex. *Definitely not the outdoor pool,* she thought, pushing the entrance door open. Once more, she enjoyed the feeling of fresh cool air swirling around her. Closing her eyes, she savoured the sensation before opening them and moving closer to the pool. Without realising, her eyes widened at the thirty-metre pool with roped off lanes and the very welcome sight of the square artesian passive pool.

That's it, she thought. *That's what I've come here for.* She put her bag on the poolside lounge chair, slipped her shoes underneath it and, taking off her towelling robe, casually placed that next to her bag.

It was only as Georgia moved towards the square passive pool that she realised there were other people in there. A family of five was watching her but showing nothing more than polite interest as they sat on its far side, almost hidden by the island bench in its centre. She smiled at them as she entered the water and allowed the feeling of bliss to show on her face.

"Yes, isn't it great?" the young mum asked her. "Especially after the drive to get here. We saw you come in. The heat looked like it really gave you a whack when you got out of the car. Did you have a long drive?"

"Oh, yes, this is so good," Georgia replied. "Just what I needed. Think it was a bit over four hours, maybe five. I wasn't taking much notice of the time, more looking around at the countryside and where I was going. I've been stuck in the city for far too long, so I enjoyed the drive. But you're right, I wasn't ready for the heat when I got out of the car.

"What about you? Have you come far for this? Oh, it's just so good." Georgia sank to her shoulders in the hot water before moving closer to the family and then perching herself on the underwater ledge.

"We're just over two hours from here. Boyd's a doctor. This is his weekend off, and we wanted to get out of town and have a break with just us and the kids. We come here whenever we can. It's perfect for us. But we've got to go and feed the hungry hordes, so we'll leave you in peace. Enjoy it. See you around." The family slowly walked up and along the ramp out of the pool, collected their belongings and left Georgia to the peace and tranquillity she hadn't realised she'd been longing for. Later, when she reluctantly forced herself to leave the relaxing warm water, Georgia slowly dried off as she looked over at the gym and its equipment. Knowing that she'd been sitting for most of the day, she pulled shorts and a tee-shirt over her bathers, slid her shoes on, and took a gym towel out of her bag. A thirty-min-ute circuit, she decided, sipping from her water bottle, following that with another decision to order room service.

Georgia had just finished drying her hair after her shower when the knock on the door indicated her meal had arrived. Checking the peephole, she opened the door to find the younger lady from reception with her dinner.

"We saw you go over to the pool earlier." She grinned at Georgia as she entered the suite. "Hope you don't mind, but I've put a prosecco piccolo on your tray. You don't have to have it, I can take it back with me, but I thought it might help you wind down after your drive and the heat." Her big brown eyes smiled up at Georgia as she gently placed the tray on the table. "I'm Janice, by the way, and I hope you don't mind about the wine." She looked back at Georgia to find her smiling.

"Janice, that's lovely, thank you so much. I'm so exhausted I never thought about a nice wine with my dinner. This will be great; please leave it with me. I just know I'm going to enjoy it." Janice nodded. "Happy to do that. I see you've booked with us for another couple of nights. Did you know we have our art show opening tomorrow night? That might be something you'd like to go to. We have some great artists out this way, and I like to promote our local events to our guests whenever I get the opportunity. It's at our cultural centre just off the main street—very easy to find, and there is a flyer in your information folder. Anyway, enjoy your dinner. I'm sure you'll sleep well after your swim this afternoon. See you around." With that, she turned to leave.

"Janice, thank you so much. I really do appreciate this and you're right, I am interested in the art show. Will you be there?" Janice nodded.

"Good, I'll see you there. I'm Georgia, and thanks again. I was not expecting such thoughtful hospitality. See you tomorrow night, if not before." Georgia closed the door, making sure it was locked, and sat down at the small table ready to enjoy her dinner and the sparkling wine.

Opening her eyes, Georgia smiled as she listened to the cheerful warbling of magpies outside her window. In the distance, a dog barked. She stretched slowly before rolling over to look at the red glowing numbers of the clock radio on the bedside table. *Huh*, she thought, *7:40? Already? Wow, I haven't slept in this late since ... since I don't know when. Well, so what, who cares?* Deciding to go for a walk and check out some of the nearby surroundings, she quickly showered and dressed before moving into the suite's kitchenette. Opening the fridge door, she removed the oranges she'd automatically put in before going to bed.

After slicing them in half, Georgia took the electric juicer and a tall glass from the overhead cupboard before firmly placing the first orange half on the juicer. Its humming was a routine part of her day, although at home this happened much earlier and a lot faster.

Pouring the fresh juice into the glass over a couple of ice cubes and lightly crushed mint leaves picked from the small pot on the window ledge, Georgia took a deep breath before opening the door and peering outside. Jet sprinklers were splashing water over the rich green lawns and, as she watched, they automatically turned off and retreated below its surface. The magpies she'd heard carolling earlier walked decisively over the thick damp green grass, sharp eyes carefully focused as they searched for grubs, worms, or any other wriggly creatures that might be unlucky enough to be caught and eaten.

Superb fairy wrens flitted in and out of the hedge lining the motel's fence, their chirping bringing another smile to Georgia's face. *How beautiful,* she thought. *I don't get to see any of this at home.* The realisation saddened her. *How much of nature's beauty have I missed because of my career?* she wondered. *A career I don't even enjoy anymore*—what? Where did that come from? Shaking her head, Georgia closed the door and walked back into the kitchenette. She rinsed her glass and the juicer before moving into the luxurious bathroom she'd hardly appreciated the night before.

"Sunscreen, hat, sunnies. All done and ready to go, if it's not too hot," Georgia muttered, making sure she had the suite's key card, her car keys, phone, and wallet tucked into her small shoulder bag before walking out into the bright sunlight.

Okay, not too hot, she thought, walking towards the motel's exit. *Half an hour or so, then a sit in the pool and then I'll go for breakfast. Well, brunch I suppose, back home it'd be brunch at that time.* With a careless shrug of her shoulders, Georgia turned left as she reached the footpath. This time it was the quiet that embraced her. No city traffic. No rushing pedestrians—*No, not here,* she thought as she recalled yesterday's elderly couple crossing the road. *They even waved at me,* she thought, remembering she'd waved back before realising what she was doing. And that felt good— nice, friendly, not like in the city. Even though she knew a few of her neighbours in the high-rise complex she lived in, it didn't have that sense of friendliness. *It's more casual here, more relaxed. Or am I more casual? I feel more relaxed.* Her eyes roamed as she walked away from the commercial area, moving into a well-maintained residential area.

They do love their trees and gardens out here, Georgia thought as she took in the manicured lawns, carefully placed shrubs, colourful garden beds, and large feature pots with plants and flowers spilling out of them. *Hanging baskets; they're stunning. It feels like I'm in a TV garden show.* Then she stopped just before her mind exploded.

This is it. This is what I want, it's perfect. It's me.No. Stop this now, she ordered her mind. *Just stop. You're tired. You're exhausted. It's holiday fever. That's all. Turn around now and go and get some coffee into your system. That's it; that's what it is. You haven't had a coffee today. Withdrawal—that's what it is.* But before she turned around to go back to the motel, Georgia reached for her phone to take a photo of the *For Sale* sign in front of the most beautiful cottage-style home she'd ever seen. *Coffee—I need coffee* became her new mantra as she marched back to her accommodation. *No swim—not just now. Coffee first, then I'll … coffee, coffee, coffee.* Georgia carefully parked the Audi a short walk from the coffee shop she'd seen the day before. *Inside, I think,* she thought as she looked at the pretty flowers in the vases on the outdoor tables. *Inside. I don't want to be on show out here.* She smiled as she felt the cool embrace of air conditioning and the welcome aroma of much-needed coffee greet her.

"Good morning," Georgia replied when the barista smiled and nodded. "Could I get a mug of flat white and a menu, please?" Then, as her eyes moved across the specials board, she spoke again, "No, sorry, I've decided already.

It'll be the smashed avo on sourdough with a medium-hard poached egg. That'll hit the spot." She read the name badge as she reached out to pay with her plastic card. "Thanks, Debbie. I'm Georgia. Is it okay if I grab the window seat?"

"Sure thing, Georgia. Welcome to Take-a-Break. I'll bring your coffee over in a tic and your brekky won't be long. Make yourself comfy; today's paper's on the rack if you'd like to flick through that while you wait."

Still smiling, Georgia carried the morning paper to her table and glanced at the headlines on the front page. Politicians, cost of living and interest rate rise details, gossip about some minor television celebrity, references to at least one overseas conflict. *Who really reads this stuff,* she wondered. *You did,* her mind replied. *You always checked this every day. You had to know this stuff back then. Whoa,* Georgia thought. *"Back then"? What? Is last week "back then"? What is this—a holiday revolution or something?* She quickly refolded the paper before placing it across the table from her.

"There's never anything cheerful in there, hey?" Debbie said as she placed the steaming mug of coffee on the table. "Would you like me to put it back, Georgia? I only get a copy for our older customers who like to have a bit of a read and look busy while they wait for others to turn up. Here's Nev—he usually has a flick through while he chats away. Morning, Nev," she continued as Georgia nodded and smiled. "Here's your paper; Georgia's finished with it." Debbie placed it on the table in front of the elderly man as he sat down nearby. "The usual, Nev?" she asked as she walked back to the coffee machine.

"Thanks, Deb." He nodded and then turned his attention to Georgia. "Hello, love—sure you've finished with this?" he asked as he smiled at her.

"Yes, thank you. It might be called the newspaper but there's nothing new there—it's all same old, same old, just different names, faces, places, and days." She grinned at him, wondering where that had come from.

"True, very true, but there is comfort in that same old, same old." His eyes twinkled across the table at her. "Could be worse, you know—could be worse." "You're right there." Debbie joined in as she put Nev's coffee on the table and then placed Georgia's breakfast order in front of her. "Sometimes the same old, same old is much better than the floods or bushfire reports we've had over the last couple of summers."

"That's so true," Georgia agreed before deciding to change the subject. "Oh, this looks beautiful, Debbie. Almost too pretty to eat." She quickly took a photo of her attractively plated breakfast garnished with edible flowers. "I'll send this to my friends at work—they'll be so envious." She smiled at the others before picking up her cutlery.

"And where'd work be, love?" Nev asked, enjoying the sight of the attractive young lady heartily tucking into her breakfast.

"Right in the middle of Sydney," she replied, carefully pushing the food into her cheek as she spoke. "This is so quiet and peaceful, so relaxing. Almost as soon as I arrived yesterday, I was up to my shoulders in the artesian water, and it was so hard to get back out. The heat's a bit much, though—no humidity, so I really felt it. This morning seemed so much better." She smiled at him as she continued eating.

"Yes, I can see you'd notice a bit of difference between the city and here," he said thoughtfully. "It's a nice town, a good community. Lots of opportunities here, you know," he said as he looked directly into her eyes. "You'll enjoy relaxing here. Now"—he sat up straighter and pointed a finger at her—"tonight. Tonight's the opening of our art show. If you're not busy, how would you like to come along with me? I can introduce you to some of the artists and other locals. Debbie'll vouch for me; I'm a good, solid, trustworthy citizen, aren't I Deb?" He wiggled his eyebrows at Georgia before looking over at the barista, who chuckled back at him.

"That's what he keeps telling us, Georgia," she said with a laugh. "And Nev's reputation as our newly retired mayor keeps him in good stead. You'd be right with him, and I can tell you now, he'll be looking forward to escorting a lovely lady like yourself to the art show. If you're not busy, go on, have a night out. I'll be there, and look—here's Gemma already. Gem works here when she's not away at uni, and she's also one of our local artists. Some of her work's on display, and it's very popular, too."

"Hi, Nev. Hi, Deb. Hello." She nodded to Georgia. "Yes, I have a couple of pieces of work on display, and thanks for those nice words, Deb. How are you, Nev? All sorted out with your usual?"

"Hello, Gemma; I'm Georgia, and this is the second time the art show's been mentioned. Janice from my motel talked about it last night and said she'd be there, too. It sounds interesting, and yes, Nev, I think it'd be nice to be escorted by one of the local celebrities." She grinned at him. "What time will I meet you there?"

His shrewd eyes gleamed as he nodded at her. *Canny girl,* he thought. "How about I meet you on the cultural centre steps about seven-thirty? The official opening is at eight, and I can introduce you around a bit before we go in. And then you'll have plenty of time to look around and socialise if you'd like to. How's that sound?"

"Lovely, thanks, Nev. I'm looking forward to it already. Janice said there was a flyer in the motel's welcome pack, but can I get one in any of the shops? Oh, thanks, Gemma." She smiled as Gemma picked one up from the counter and waved it before bringing it to her. "You didn't have to do that, I could have grabbed it on my way out, but thanks so much." Putting her knife and fork down, Georgia began reading.

Nev waited until she finished reading before speaking again. "So, Georgia, how about I sit with you while you finish your coffee, and you can tell me a bit about yourself? That way I'll know who I'm introducing to our locals tonight."

When she nodded, Nev stood up and moved over to her table. "Rightio," he started, "so I'm a long-term local; my family moved here when I was a kid. Went to school here. Moved to Sydney for my vet studies and, when I graduated, moved back and started working. My daughter and son-in-law run the practice now—they're both vets— and I have a couple of nieces working with them as vet nurses. They're getting busier and busier. Don't s'pose you're a vet, are you? Didn't think so," he replied when she shook her head. "Probably not much call for vets in inner Sydney and your nails are much longer than all my girls'," he said with a grin.

"You're pretty observant, Nev," Georgia replied. "I'm a lawyer. On leave. I've got just over four weeks left and I'm just cruising around for the first couple then I'm thinking about heading up to Cairns and the Reef for a week. I didn't realise how exhausted I am until last night when I sank into that beautifully hot water. I slept like a log, too. So, a few days here just doing nothing much and enjoying an art show opening sounds pretty good. What other local attractions or events would you recommend?"

"That'd mainly depend on your interests, love," he replied thoughtfully. "There's a pretty decent walking track through the park right along the side of the creek that runs through town before it joins the river. If you go into the centre of the park you'll find our Indigenous Art Trail, that's fairly new and it's growing. It's very popular with visitors and most locals." He grinned at the surprised look on her face.

"Yeah, like most other communities, we have a few small-minded people who don't or won't or can't recognise the importance of Aboriginal culture and heritage, but having said that, they don't seem to cause any trouble. They just whinge and carry on every now and then and the rest of us tend to ignore them. Our local races are coming up Saturday. Any chance of you still being here for that? It's always a good day with a bit of fun, fashions on the field, a ladies' luncheon, and a concert that night. Oh, and the Saturday afternoon after that there's a Cancer Council high tea and fashion parade out at one of the local homesteads. While the homestead's not open to the public, its gardens are, and they're worth a look. They've featured on TV a couple of times. You've chosen a good time to visit us, Georgia. How does all that sound?"

Georgia leaned back in her seat, lifted her coffee to her lips, and looked thoughtfully at him, her mind racing as she tried to absorb all this information. She blinked when she realised he hadn't stopped and was continuing with the local itinerary.

"And then, if you like a bit of outdoor activity, a couple of our locals have just started kayak river tours. I was one of their first customers and can really recommend that. Seeing the area from the middle of the river's pretty good, and none of us know why it wasn't thought of years ago. Of course, there's fishing, and if you go out to the wetlands, there're some great bird-spotting places. You could be as busy and as active as you like while you're here. But it sounds to me that you just need to rest and relax, so, if you're interested in a half-day spa treatment …" He winked and grinned at the surprise on Georgia's face.

"Retired mayor, remember? I've still got my finger on the pulse and have a bit of an idea about what's popular. We've got a couple of great beauty treatment places just down the street, as well as one that's only a few minutes out of town, situated right near the riverbank. There's also golf, tennis, and tomorrow we have our seniors' social morning. Later in the week, there's night-time barefoot bowls with a barbecue tea. Hitting targets yet, Georgia? You can always go clay target shooting and the archery club's having an open day later this month. The council pool has aqua aerobics in the mornings and a couple of nights a week and the library has an activities program that you might like to have a look at. Now, a lawyer, you said?" Nev continued. "Our local radio station might like to have a chat with you about a half-hour segment later in the week. Is that something you'd be interested in finding a little bit more about? Would you like to give me your mobile number and I'll get in touch with Stella, our morning announcer, to see if she'd like to get in touch with you?" And almost before she knew what was happening, Georgia had given her closely guarded mobile number to a man she'd just met. She shook her head in disbelief.

"Whoa, Nev—I think you might need to slow down a bit," Debbie called out. "The poor girl's looking a bit overwhelmed. But he is right, Georgia, there's a lot happening around here, and it's pretty much always like this. Okay, we don't have the races or the high teas every week, but we are an active community, and we all get in and support everything that's on. That's why our art show is on everyone's radar just now. It'll be good to see you there with Nev tonight, and look, Nev, here's your morning crew coming in."

"Good morning, Jack, Bill, Fred—go and meet Georgia. Nev's just overwhelmed her with details of all the local events that are coming up and I think she needs rescuing. So go and say hello now and you'll be able to catch up with her tonight at the art show. Nev's offered to escort her in and introduce her to more of the locals. Look out, Georgia—you're about to be invaded." She smiled as she waved the three elderly, well-dressed gentlemen over to her table. *Hah!* Georgia chuckled to herself. *Haven't been in town a day and I've met more men this morning than in the last eight months at home.* She smiled broadly at the gents as they pulled out chairs and made themselves comfortable. "Good morning, everyone. I'm Georgia, and I'm on holidays and visiting your lovely town for a few days." She picked up her coffee cup as her fascination with her new breakfast buddies grew.

The four men laughed as they reminisced about previous art shows and some of the more eccentric local artists and their work.

Bill chuckled as he described the first year that an anonymous artist section was included. "The only stipulation was that the artwork had to be socially acceptable. It could be any medium and any topic or theme. Some of the young farmers got together and welded rusty wire, old tools, horseshoes, and car and truck bits and pieces into some kind of statue that they called … what was it, Fred? Whirlwind? Cyclone? Oh, something like that. Anyway, while most of us thought it was a tangled jumble of a mess, somehow they got the numbers and won People's Choice Award. They were so surprised they donated it on the spot to the council for one of the parks. You should have seen Nev's face. He'd just become mayor at that time and spoke most politely about the creativity of the farming community and how their Whirlwind could be seen as representing the turmoil of past, present, and future agricultural life. Nev's always had a way with words, hasn't he?" The men nodded and grinned.

"And that began a local tradition. Since then, every artist who's won the anonymous artist section has donated their work to the council. We've got paintings, sculptures, tapestries, mosaics, you name it, placed in and around town."

Nev grinned at the look of amazement on Georgia's face. "The group actually called their work *Hurricane*, and that's a story in itself. They meant to call it *Turbulence* after the song about a bull rider, but somehow in all the excitement got themselves mixed up and gave it the wrong name, which we stuck to because it's such a great story.

That'd have to be at least fifteen years ago now. Most of those blokes should be there tonight. They've never created another artwork, though; they say they're resting on their laurels.

"You know," he mused, "we should mention that it'll be *Hurricane*'s twentieth anniversary soon and they should celebrate that with another creation. That'd get their brains and welders working, I reckon."

The four elderly faces lit up at this suggestion and Georgia felt that, after the official opening of the art show, the men would follow through on it. She laughed quietly at the thought and then, having finished her breakfast and coffee, thanked them for being such great company and promised to catch up with them that night.

"Debbie, that was the best breakfast I've had in ages," she called as she moved towards the doorway. "Thanks so much for introducing me to those lovely men. I'm really looking forward to tonight. See you then." She waved to the men before heading back out to her car knowing that she had the biggest smile plastered all over her face.

Before she realised, Georgia had driven past her motel and turned down the same street she'd walked along earlier in the morning. Parking in the shade of a large jacaranda tree, she gazed once more at the *For Sale* sign outside the home she'd fallen in love with.

This is ridiculous, she told herself. *I know nothing about this town, except that some of its people are friendly and welcoming. What am I thinking? Yes, I might be able to afford it, but what on earth would I do here?Find out,* a little voice inside her head replied. *Go on; research the town, the district, and find out just what you could do here.* "Ridiculous," she said out loud. "Just ridiculous. Anyway, I'm going for a swim. That'll sort my head out."

Back in her motel suite, even though Georgia had intended to change straight into her bathers, she found herself at her laptop researching the town and local district, or the local government area, as these were now all called.

Hmm, just over fifteen thousand in town and almost forty-five thousand in the shire. I didn't realise it's this big. Or small. She grinned thinking of Sydney city and its greater population area."OMG," she said aloud. "There's a job. For me. Oh boy, oh boy." And before she could do anything else, she closed the laptop, went into the bathroom, and changed into her bathers. "Swim. I'm going for a swim. I'm going to do laps." She checked her bag, making sure her goggles were there before smoothing sunscreen lotion on her face, arms, and legs. Grabbing her beach towel and room keycard, she slipped into an oversized T-shirt, slid on her sandals, and tried to focus her thoughts on swimming instead of a dream home with a beautiful garden and a new job in a town she'd been in for just one day.

For the rest of the day, Georgia focused her thoughts on resting and relaxing. Each time her thoughts wandered to the house or the possibility of a job, she refocused on an art opening or a light exercise program or reading at least one of the books she'd packed. Deciding it was far too hot to walk in the afternoon, Georgia retreated to the lounge chairs on the shady lawn with her book and bottle of cold water. However, the antics of the little blue wrens darting in and out of the hedge captivated her attention. Going back to her room, she grabbed the art bag she'd thrown into the car as a last-minute thought. Checking that her supplies were all there, she went back to her shady spot and opened the sketch book. Selecting a pencil and making sure the sharpener and eraser were handy, Georgia began sketching the background of the hedge, the ornamental fencing, and then started to draw a couple of wrens. Immersed in her work, she wasn't aware that Janice had walked over to her until she coughed lightly.

"I'm sorry to interrupt you, Georgia," Janice said when Georgia looked around in surprise. "I noticed you've been over here for some time and I'm about to knock off. I just wanted to check that you're still going to the art show tonight. There's plenty of time yet, but I didn't want you to feel rushed once the sun starts going down. Also, I don't know if you've heard, but there's always a nice supper after the official part of the evening, so you might not want to have too much to eat before you get there. Anyway, I'm sorry to interrupt, but I know what it's like once I start drawing—time just gets away. You *are* still going tonight, aren't you? Good," Janice said when Georgia nodded, "I'll see you then. Enjoy the rest of the afternoon." She waved cheerfully as she walked back towards the main office.

"Janice!" Georgia called after her. Janice stopped and turned around. "Thanks so much for that. I hadn't realised that it's getting late. I really appreciate it. I didn't know about the supper, and I had a lovely breakfast this morning." She stood up and walked across to Janice. "I met Nev and three other fellows at the coffee shop and had the best time. I'm really looking forward to tonight, but can I ask—just how formal will it be? With what I brought with me, I won't be overdressed, but I don't want to be underdressed, either. Have you got a couple of minutes? Could you come and have a look at what I've brought and give me some ideas? In Sydney I'd be right, I'd be able to frock up with the best of them, but I don't want to turn up looking like it's not an important event. Especially as Nev's going to take me inside and introduce me around." She grinned at the surprised look on Janice's face.

"You look just as surprised as I felt," Georgia said. "I've never been asked out over breakfast before, but Debbie vouched for him and the three friends of his who joined us were so funny. They reminded me of some of my uncles. I don't think I've laughed so much for ages. And so now I don't want to let them down by being too casually dressed. And I hear you're one of the artists, too, so I want don't want to let you down, either. Have you got a few minutes?" "Sure thing, Georgia," came the reply. "Only I've never been asked about what to wear before. We just all turn up. Oh, we're not casual, but we're not over the top, either, if you know what I mean. Some of the local ladies might be in jeans, but they'll be designer jeans and look top notch. Did you bring an LBD? That'd fit in well if you did." She grinned. "There'll be LBDs, LRDs, all sorts of little coloured dresses, some with pearls, some with chains. I think you'd call tonight 'good casual'. Some of the older men will be in suits—Nev and his gang definitely will—but most of the blokes just wear good casual stuff. C'mon, let's pack your work up and go back to your suite. I just love going through other girls' clothes and stuff."

They chatted about Nev and his "gang" as they collected Georgia's bits and pieces and went back to her suite. Moving into the walk-in robe, Janice's eyes lit up. "This is perfect, Georgia," she said, lifting up a deep blue, knee-length dress. "You'll look lovely in this; the colour really suits you. Yep, this and whatever you choose to wear with it. Right, you're done. Now I've got to go and get myself organised. I'll see you there, and if you'd like to go out after supper, a few of us are heading over to the Royal. It's one of the top pubs—does great cocktails; would you like that? We usually do a bit of a critique of the night and the artwork; it's always fun. You'd be welcome, and I think you'd like the people who wander over there. Especially as I know you're an artist, too."

"Oh no, Janice," Georgia laughed. "I'm definitely not an artist. I like to sketch, that's all, and I haven't had an opportunity to for … well, for such a long time. It was a last-minute decision to throw my sketching gear into the car, and I'm so glad I did. Thanks so much for helping me choose what to wear tonight. I honestly had no idea and I'd have hated to turn up overdone. See you soon."

It felt good knowing that she'd fit in rather than stand out, Georgia thought as she locked her car and walked up to the cultural centre. Waving at Nev—and yes, he was wearing a suit—she smiled at the people gathering on the steps to the foyer.

"Ah, Georgia, my dear." Nev reached out and took her hand. "You look lovely. I'm so glad you're here. The boys are coming up from the car park now and are keen to catch up with you again. I'm sure you're going to enjoy tonight. It's not really that sophisticated," he said with a grin, "but it's one of our nice local get-togethers that we all enjoy. Okay"—he nodded at Jack, Bill, and Fred, who were coming towards them—"the gang's all here; let's go in and see what's what in our little world of art."

As they walked inside, Georgia was stunned. As well as people everywhere, the wall hangings and displays of various forms of artwork were incredible. Even at first glance, she could see the organisation behind the exhibition. Pottery and statuary were creatively sited in and around the displays of paintings. Instinctively, she moved towards the monochromes, momentarily forgetting Nev, who indulgently followed with his gang. "She's hooked, I think," he said softly. "Let's see what she says."

"Oh, Nev," she sighed. "Look at the form, the texture, the shading, I just love this," she said as she stood almost awestruck in front of a scene of an abandoned farmhouse. "The detail is superb. Do you know if it's for sale? Are any of the works here on sale?"

"Here, Georgia," Fred replied, holding out a catalogue. "I noticed you hadn't seen these, so I grabbed a couple. We're really only here to look, you know—'bums on seats' sort of thing—and I bet Nev here wouldn't have thought you'd be looking at buying anything tonight. Sometimes we reckon he's forgotten he retired. He enjoys promoting our events and making sure that as many people as possible come along. Think he struck a winner with you, did he, love?"

"Fred, you're right," she said, nodding. "I don't know what I was expecting, but it certainly wasn't work like this." She gazed around. "There must be an incredible amount of talent in and around your town." Her eyes returned to the scene in front of her. "This just sings to me. I'll have to find out if it is for sale. If not, I wonder if I could commission another one from the artist. Are the details in the catalogue?" Her hands itched to get hold of it. One part of her mind was amazed; she'd never responded to any piece of art the way she had with this.

"Yes, love," Fred replied. "Here it is—number twenty-six. Oh, of course. We should have known. Why didn't you know, Nev?" he asked with a grin. "It's one of Justin's. He's quite well known around these parts. Exhibits in Sydney and Brisbane, even had a couple of shows on the Gold Coast in the last few years. He'll be around somewhere. Now, let's see if we can spot him—he's tall enough, we should be able to."

"Just over there, Fred," Bill broke in as he indicated a group of people standing near the stage. "Looks like the officials are about to get started. Let's grab a seat. Where would you like to sit, love?" he asked Georgia. "You choose. If we leave it to Nev, he'll be centre front." He pretended to elbow Nev, who chuckled in response.

"That's only because we're all half-deaf, you know," he replied. "Come along, Georgia—let's go find somewhere unobtrusive but where we can keep an eye on Justin so we can introduce you and then you can talk about the piece you like."

Nodding her agreement and waving across the room to Janice and her group of friends, Georgia indicated a section of chairs close by. "Those should do, shouldn't they? Close enough to see and hear and still close to that stunning sketch." She let herself be guided to a section where, for the first time, she could see the artist himself. *Wow*, she thought. *He's handsome. And talented.* Settling herself, she was ready to hear speeches from people she didn't know about artists she didn't know and a town and its community she also knew little to nothing about. While she wasn't going to allow herself to be bored, Georgia didn't think she'd be as entertained as she was. The master of ceremonies spoke informatively and entertainingly about previous art exhibitions and the quality of the work. The MC then invited the local member of parliament to open the exhibition and Georgia was pleased to hear another short and entertaining address.

Once the formalities were over, some people who'd chosen to sit began moving while many others stayed seated, talking with friends as drinks and nibblies were served.

"Thanks, Sophie," Nev said as he took a glass of sparkling wine and raised his eyebrows at Georgia, who nodded as she took it from him. "Soph, this is Georgia—she's visiting and came along to have a look at our local creativity. What have you got on display this year?" Turning to Georgia, he continued, "Sophie's one of our high school captains and has been exhibiting for what, three years now?" The young girl nodded. "Lovely to meet you, Georgia. Thanks, Nev. Yes, I've got a couple of watercolours in this year. Been too busy to do much else, and they'll be part of my Year 12 portfolio. Miss Andrews doesn't mind that they're on display here before the school's exhibition next month. I think she's hoping I can produce another one or two before then, but I'm doubtful. This is a busy year, and—guess what?" she playfully asked the older men who weren't able to answer before she rushed on. "I got my driver's licence this afternoon. I drove Mum and Dad here tonight. They pretended to be scared, but we all know I've been behind the wheel on the farm for years. It's good that I can now officially go out on the road. Oops, did I say that out loud?" She laughed as she moved onto another group with her tray of drinks.

"Well, that's one incredibly confident and beautiful young lady," Georgia said. "School captain, experienced artist, new driver, and an exuberant waiter as well. What's in the water here, Nev? Is everyone here like her—talented, confident, outgoing? I know I've only been here five minutes, but I feel like I'm surrounded by creativity and confidence. Janice from my motel reception is similar with her confidence and talent. I must catch up with her. She's invited me to the Royal—is that right?—the Royal Hotel for drinks and a bit more socialising when this is finished. I think I'd like to do that, too. This is all so different from Sydney—all I seem to have done over the last few years is work, work, and more work."

"Well, Georgia, you're here now, and we'll help you relax," Bill said, looking down at her. "I think it'll do you a bit of good to hit our little night lights with Janice and her group. They're a great group of young people; you'll have fun with them, and they're not into anything silly. Nev would know if they were, and he'd be quietly steering you in another direction. Wouldn't you, Nev?"

"Yes, that's right, Bill. But we've got to remember we were all young once, too. I seem to recall sharing a bit of mischief now and then with you and others. But no names, no pack drill. Now, not changing the subject, Georgia, but here's someone I'd like you to meet. Justin, got a minute, mate? This is Georgia—she's visiting town, and Janice and I both asked her to come along. There's one of your pieces that's caught her eye. Georgia, this is Justin Watterson, one of our artists and also one of our local graziers." He stopped, looked more closely at them both, gave his head a slight shake and continued, "Well, Fred and the boys and me, we've got a few people we need to catch up with. Georgia, if I don't see you before you head off with Janice, then maybe I'll see you for coffee in the morning. Same time, same place, same table." He leaned forward, touched her on the hand and then gathered up his gang and left. "Pleased to meet you, Georgia. So, you're visiting. Where do you hail from?" Justin asked as he looked down at one of the most attractive faces he'd seen for a long time. "And can I ask how long are you staying?"

"I'm not sure, Justin," she replied. "I'm on leave from my work in Sydney and, apart from resting and relaxing, I don't have any real plans. Now, Nev said that number twenty-six—the abandoned cottage—is one of your pieces. Is it for sale? And what's the process of buying any of the work tonight? Who do I see about that? I should have asked Nev, but everything just seemed to happen so quickly: seeing your work, then the speeches and the opening, and now he's moved off to see other people. That shouldn't surprise me," she added. "He obviously knows just about everyone here." She smiled up at the man she'd originally thought handsome.

Hmm, more than that, she thought as their eyes connected.

"Right—" Justin cleared his throat. "Right, Georgia, have you got a catalogue? In the back, there's a page of sticky dots. Write your initials on one of them and then lightly stick that on the frame of the piece or pieces you'd like. It's pretty much first claim if you feel the price is okay. If you'd like to claim this before you look around, then I'll help with that. I'd be happy to walk around with you seeing that Nev's shot through." He glanced around. "Then, if there are any other pieces you like, I might be able to introduce you to the artists. We all know each other." As Georgia took her pen from her bag, Justin waved over to the table where the designated clerks were busy at work. He quickly pointed to Georgia and then the work she was interested in and nodded. A quick wave indicated his message was clear. The work was hers. No-one else had a chance at number twenty-six.

As Georgia finished placing her sticky green dot on the frame of the abandoned cottage, she heard a quiet laugh as she was hugged. Surprised, she looked around. "Janice, it's great to see you," Georgia said as she hugged her new friend back. "This is wonderful. What a lovely evening, although I haven't gotten very far. Do you know Justin? Of course you do." She grinned as they both nodded. "I think, or I hope, I've just claimed this. Now I want to see your work—lead me to it. And what about you, Justin, are you able to come too?" He smiled in agreement and, with Janice leading, they walked over to the other side of the hall.

"Oh, Janice, this is gorgeous," Georgia said softly as she stared at the watercolour painting of the house she'd seen that morning and more than once had thought of as hers. Tears came into her eyes. *If I can't have the house, I can always have the painting,* she thought.

"I've seen this house; I walked past it this morning before I went for coffee. It's beautiful, and you've captured it perfectly." Without another thought, Georgia reached back into her bag for her pen and wrote her initials on another sticky green dot.

"Thanks, Georgia. It was my grandmother's. She passed away a few months ago and the family is now ready to part with it. We can't keep it. We've taken everything that we wanted, as she told us to. And now it's up for sale. Nan said that there would be someone who'd feel it was right for them and they'd come along when the time was right. So, we're just looking after it now. We take turns in mowing and one of my cousins is a landscaper. He just loves taking care of the gardens and plants. But he's got his own place out of town, so this is sort of a hobby for him until it's sold.

"I've made sure that everyone in the family has their own copy of one of my paintings of the house. This was the last one. For some reason I lost count so thought I'd display it here tonight. Apart from the family ones, this is a one-off, and they're all slightly different. I know," she said with a laugh. "Too much information. It just all came out when I saw you claiming it. Oh, look," she continued. "Some of the group are heading off already." She looked at her watch. "Oh, it's later than I thought. What would you like to do, Georgia? Are you ready to leave, or would you like to look around a bit more?" "Janice, if you'd like to leave now, I can bring Georgia over to the Royal in a little while—if you'd like to stay and look around, that is," Justin said, looking at her. "There's another half-hour or so before tonight closes, but the display will be open for the next week. And you should really speak to our clerks about your purchases before you leave tonight. How does all that sound to both of you? Right," he continued as they both nodded. "I'm happy to walk around with you, Georgia, and Nev and the others are still over there. Apart from being in helping to hang pieces yesterday and today, I haven't had a good look around yet, either. So, we'll see you in a little while, Janice, if you'd like to head off."

He didn't miss the way she looked at Georgia, almost as if asking if she'd be okay. Knowing that Nev and the gang were still around helped Georgia make up her mind. "Yes, that sounds like a good idea, Janice. I know you've been working all day, it's about time you relaxed, too. If you're happy to show me where the Royal is, Justin, that would be nice. I'll see you in a little while, Janice, and like I said earlier, I'm really looking forward to socialising, too. See you soon." The girls hugged before Janice went back to her friends. "Justin, I'm thinking that a quick walk around would be nice." Georgia smiled up at him. "I'd like to see as much as I can tonight, but I can spend more time in here over the next couple of days. It's probably more important to finalise my claims tonight so the clerks can leave. Does that sound okay to you?"

"That's all good with me," he replied knowing that many pairs of eyes had been watching them throughout the evening. "Now, let's move over to the oil paintings. Some of the artists are still there, and you might like to say hello to them. I'm pretty sure they'd enjoy meeting you. Some of them are absolute darlings; quite a few of our seniors have been painting for decades and always produce great work. Ladies—" He nodded to a group he knew had been keeping their eyes on them for a little while. "—I'd like you to meet Georgia. She's visiting and Nev and Janice invited her along tonight. Georgia, this is Maisie, Betty, Dorothy, Gwen, and Ellen. They're all locals and have been exhibiting since our first art show. There's quite a lot of talent in this small group," he added. "Gwen, you've won prizes in the Royal Shows in Sydney and Adelaide, haven't you?" She smiled and nodded. "And Maisie, you've won awards up and down the coast?" She also smiled and nodded. "Dorothy's work is on display in Parliament House and the state library and, Ellen, you and Betty have work in regional and interstate galleries, is that right?"

Georgia shook her head in wonderment. "Hello, ladies," she replied. "Earlier, I asked Nev if there was something in the water around here. Compared to Sydney, this is a small town; it doesn't have a big population, but goodness me, the creativity and the talent that's on display here tonight. It's all just so lovely." She continued as they all smiled at her. "It's not just in the artwork; the homes, the gardens, and the people ... wow, I've never come across anything like this in Sydney. Although I'm sure there'd have to be pockets of it, scattered around the harbour and up in the mountains. But to have all this"—she waved her hand around her—"concentrated in the one place; I'm just amazed." She came to a stop, feeling the eyes and ears that were focused directly on her. "I'm sorry," she said as she felt the warmth steal up over her face. "I'm rambling.""No, you're not dear," replied one of the ladies—Gwen, or was it Maisie? Georgia couldn't quite remember. "You've just given us all a lovely compliment, so thank you for that. Now, of course, you're the young lady who had breakfast with Nev and his gang this morning. They're a great bunch, but maybe you'd like to have a bit of time being not so overwhelmed. If you'd like to, and only if you'd like to, we're having a book chat and afternoon tea at the aged care residence tomorrow afternoon at one o'clock if you'd like to come along.

"There's a newly published author who's coming to talk about her book; it's an Australian historical novel. I haven't finished my copy yet, but I am enjoying it. You'd be very welcome to join us, if that's something you'd be interested in." As Georgia looked into the faded blue eyes of someone who suddenly reminded her of her gran, she nodded.

"Yes, thanks, Maisie—you are Maisie, aren't you?" The sweet, wrinkled face smiled back at her. "I think I'd like to go to that, it does sound interesting, and I do love a good Aussie novel, and it's important to support our writers just as much as our artists. Thank you. One o'clock, you said?" Again, heads nodded and faces smiled at her. "I'll see you then. And now, I'm off to the Royal to catch up with Janice and her group. You know"—Georgia leaned towards the older ladies with a twinkle in her eye—"I haven't been out and about so much for a long time. In Sydney, all I seemed to be doing was work, work, and more work, and now, since being here, I've realised … oops, anyway, I must be off. I'll see you tomorrow."

Trying not to shake her head as she walked over to the clerks and their administration papers, Georgia also bit her lip. *Goodness me girl*, she thought. *What were you about to tell them? That almost overnight you've decided that you don't like your job, you don't like your work, you don't like your city lifestyle—what on earth has gotten into you?'*

"Hello." Georgia smiled at the casually dressed but official-looking young lady behind the table that was being used as a desk. "I'm Georgia, and I hope I've claimed numbers twenty-six and seventy-five."

"Hi, Georgia. I'm Crystal and, yes, you're almost the lucky new owner of Justin and Janice's works. You've got a good eye on you, and you sure were lucky to get in so quickly. Are you new in town? I don't think I've seen you around." Crystal burst into a wide grin. "There you go, Georgia, that's me being a sticky-beak. I'm still fairly new myself. I manage the supermarket, so I've gotten to know most of the people and faces in and around town. But let's get back to the paperwork for you." Crystal touched a few keys on the computer keyboard and the printer sprang to life.

"Here's your invoice," she said, passing the sheet of paper to Georgia, who found herself trying to keep up. "Now," Crystal continued, "we just need you to fill out these details for the receipt and insurance, and I do need to ask, would you be happy for us to put you into our database? That way we can send you information about our local activities, future art shows, other events? There's no obligation, and we do understand that many people have concerns about databases being hacked and all that sort of thing." She smiled at Georgia.

"Yes, please do that, Crystal. I don't mind being added to your database, and hackers don't really worry me too much. I've worked with far worse crooks in Sydney," she stated then giggled at what had just fallen out of her mouth. "Oops, probably I shouldn't have said that," she said, frowning, "but anyway, I did. Sorry." She realised there was more than one startled face looking at her. "I'm a lawyer, and I think I've heard all the jokes and sayings about lawyers," she explained. "It's okay—" She winked and continued, "I haven't brought any of the bad guys with me. Oh dear, that didn't sound good at all, did it?" Again, she felt a warm flush on her cheeks.

Behind her, Nev and Fred laughed out loud. "Well, Georgia," Fred said softly, "I'm so pleased to hear that after having had breakfast with you this morning. We've just popped over to say goodnight and to ask if we can share your table again tomorrow morning. After that statement of yours, we'd love to hear some of the tales of dastardly deeds from the big smoke—that you're able to share, of course. There'd be nothing like a bit of a yarn about some of those bad guys or wicked women to go with our tea and toast first thing in the morning, right, Nev?"

Both men laughed as they patted Georgia on the shoulder. "See you tomorrow, love," Nev said when Georgia nodded before they strolled off laughing.

"Here, Georgia," Crystal said as she held out two white stickers with the word *SOLD* boldly in red across the front. "We've found that a lot of new owners love putting the sold sticker on their purchases; it seems to make it real for them. Would you like to do that? Mark," she said to the tall man busily packing stationery items into a box behind them, "can you hold the fort for a moment, please? I'll just go with Georgia to put the stickers on her purchases. By the way, Georgia, this is Mark, my partner. Mark, this is Georgia."

"Great to meet you, Mark," Georgia responded as she took his outstretched hand. "This is a lovely event; I've really enjoyed it."

"It's good to meet you, too, Georgia," Mark replied as he shook her hand. "I'm pleased you've had a great night. Go and brand your new art and enjoy being its owner or custodian." He gave her a friendly smile before turning back to his work.

Justin moved back to stand next to Georgia just as she attached the "sold" sticker to the frame of his sketch. "I'm so pleased you bought my work," he said with a smile. "I like to think of it going home with you in a few days."

Georgia stopped herself from frowning. Of course she'd be going home soon. This was a brief visit, a break, a little bit of time spent here from her overall holiday time. Why then, did she feel bereft at hearing those words?

"Now, if you're ready," Justin continued, "we could start moving over to the Royal. The crowd's almost gone, and the committee workers are finishing up for the night. Their next shift starts at ten-thirty tomorrow morning, so they're ready for a good night's sleep after getting everything ready for tonight. I saw Janice and the others leave about fifteen minutes ago, so they'll just be getting comfortable."

"Thanks, Justin," she replied, still trying to overcome the despondency his words about going home had given her.

Georgia enjoyed being in the warm night air on the short walk to the Royal Hotel. "What a lovely evening," she said, looking around. "The fairy lights look so pretty in the trees, and what's that I can smell? Jasmine, isn't it? I think it's too late for wisteria—that finished flowering in Sydney a couple of weeks ago." Then she exclaimed, "Oh, look at that," as a small bat flew down and snatched a moth that had been fluttering in the streetlight. "I don't know whether to say, 'good catch bat' or 'bad luck moth', but I've never seen anything like that in Sydney. But then I've never gone out walking to a pub I haven't been to with a man I've only just met before either." Unaware of Justin's eyes on her, Georgia looked around. "This is such a lovely place. You're so lucky to live and work here, Justin."

"Yes, we all are," he replied. "It's a great community. It's also growing, slowly, but it is growing. Not like a lot of other regional towns. There's a bit of vibrancy here that doesn't seem apparent in other places up and down the highway. I'm pleased you like it, Georgia. And I'm pleased you met Nev and his gang. They'll enjoy your company while you're here," he paused. "I don't think you told me how long you're staying. Ah, here we go." He walked up the two steps to the Royal's entrance and opened the door for her.

"And there they are." Justin indicated with his head and Georgia saw Janice and a group of people seated at a long table not far from the bar. The lighting, while not dim, was not overly bright, either. And while Georgia could hear music in the background, she could also hear voices, snippets of conversation, punchlines that caused loud laughter, and some quiet laughter filtering through all the sounds. Standing still, she looked around taking it all in. Neatly dressed people all looking to be enjoying themselves, conversing in groups and communicating with smiles and waves to others.

"What would you like, Georgia?" Justin asked. "It looks like Janice and the girls are enjoying cocktails, maybe mocktails because some of her friends are nurses on the night shift and they'll be starting work soon." He smiled at Georgia's startled expression. "We're a small town, Georgia; a small community. We all know each other—we know what people do, where they work, we know people's families, often for generations. It's probably very different from what you're used to in Sydney," he added. "It certainly is, Justin," she replied. "Back there, I could never walk into a hotel and know people, let alone where they work and what they're probably drinking. This is incredibly different. Now, I think I'd like a mocktail, please. I've had a couple of long days and some very nice wine earlier. I wouldn't like to spoil it. One of those, please," she said, pointing to a glass garnished with pineapple, "but only if it's a mocktail. And I'm driving, too," she remembered. "So that'll be more than enough for me, thanks."

She continued looking around while Justin went to the bar. She watched as he and the barperson chatted while their drinks were being made. *This is all so different,* she thought, nodding back at the barperson, who smiled politely at her as he handed Justin's change back. And then, that little voice in the back of her head that had been so quiet all night whispered, *And it could be yours. You could easily become part of all of this.* Together they moved to Janice's group, where Georgia was introduced to the group, many of whom were around her age. As she chatted, Georgia realised they all had many interests in common: work commitments—and her holiday time was a cause of envy, happiness, and interest to everyone—art, music, and their local community and its events. Most of all, Georgia realised she felt welcome and at ease. This, she mused, was something she'd never experienced in Sydney. Sure, she'd attended work functions and training days where there was a common factor for everyone, but the theme of work and the sense of others' self-importance was always present. Yes, Georgia acknowledged, she was new, a curiosity, someone just as different to this group as she was to them, and feeling welcome did not automatically mean she was part of them.

That will come—in time, the little voice in the back of her head whispered. *If you would like this, if you want this, it's yours for the taking.* Again, Georgia pushed the little voice and its whispers to the back of her mind and focused on those and the conversation around her.

Later that night, as she settled into the comfort of her suite's luxurious queen-size bed, Georgia returned to the photos of the cottage she now knew had belonged to Janice's grandmother and was obviously much cherished by her family. She then turned to the job advertisement she'd seen earlier that day: here, in this town, a position for a senior and experienced lawyer. She saw that the advertisement had been online for a couple of months. *Maybe tomorrow*, she thought tiredly. *Maybe tomorrow I'll look into it.*

Again, Georgia slept later than usual but woke refreshed. Quickly she scrambled into her clothes and headed out for a morning walk, knowing where her footsteps would take her. Once more she stopped at the front of the cottage, this time reading the *For Sale* sign more carefully before continuing along the street, looking at the well-cared for homes and their attractive gardens.

It's quiet, cared for, peaceful. It's a community here, she thought as she walked along the nearby streets. I've never had this feeling in Sydney. It's always been rush, rush, rush, with no awareness of being part of a real community. I'm just part of a workplace, a work force, a work community. I need more than that, she realised, and this could be it. I think I've connected with a number of people here and I don't think it'd be hard to strengthen that. Do I want to take the plunge? If I do there's no real turning back … but there could be options.

Check out the job, apply, see if it's offered, then talk to Janice and her family about leasing the cottage and, if it all fits as well as I think I'd like, take the big steps then. It'd be easy to take leave of absence from work, they'd soon get another robot to replace me … Hell, where did that come from? Yes, Georgia thought, *that's just how I've felt and just how I've been working. Automatically. High quality automatic, but I've been a robot for a long time. It's time to find the human again.* As if in response to her thoughts, a magpie strolling across the lawn beside her carolled its joyfulness. When she entered Take-a-Break, Georgia saw that Nev and the gang were already seated and in full discussion mode. "Good morning, everyone," she said, waving at their table. She stopped at the counter to speak to Debbie and Gemma and order a light breakfast and that all-important mug of coffee. "Wasn't last night lovely? I'm still shaking my head about being the new owner of two beautiful pieces and I'm going back for another look at them after this. You know"—she smiled at the group as she sat down with them—"I didn't even take a photo of my buys last night; never thought to do that, and I can't wait to see them again. It's so exciting. Well, to me it is."

"You did look to be enjoying it, love," Nev said as he sipped his coffee and looked carefully at her. "And you seem to be very relaxed, refreshed this morning. Have you had an early morning spa treatment?" His bushy eyebrows waggled their humour at her.

"Not yet; just a gentle walk around a couple of blocks, taking in the sights and sounds. I rarely hear maggies in

Sydney and it's such a pleasure to wake up to their songs. And as for the blue wrens, seeing them just makes my day. This"—she waved her hand around the coffee shop—"all this, is so very lovely." She thanked Gemma, who placed her breakfast and coffee on the table, and then picked up her cutlery to attack the scrambled eggs on toast. "So, Georgia," Fred began, "those crooks you've worked with in the big smoke—got any tales you can tell us? I've been looking forward to hearing something about your work—what you do, what it's like, and some of the stories I'm sure you've got over the years. How long have you been practising? Well, not practising but working in your area?" His face smiled encouragingly at her.

"Now, that's a good question, Fred. Well, more than one good question, I suppose." She smiled back. "I've been working for just over eight years now, and yes, I have met more than my fair share of unsavoury characters. Most of my work's been in white collar and corporate law, but I also do some pro bono for a women's shelter and there are some very sad stories there that just don't seem to fit with this beautiful morning." The sadness in her eyes was obvious to everyone at the table.

"So," Nev said, "you're obviously experienced and, I'd say, with more than just an ordinary law degree, bet you did honours." He smiled at her.

"Wow, that's a good guess, Nev. And so long ago I've almost forgotten about it. Yes, 2A honours in Environmental Studies. If I'd pushed harder, worked harder, I might have won first class honours, but I got what I was aiming for and enjoyed my studies. So many others burnt themselves out going for that little bit extra and I saw myself in this career for the long haul. Oh, this is delicious. Not changing the subject," she quickly said as four pair of eyes settled on her, "just stating the obvious. Now, because you've asked, here's something I can talk about that happened when I first joined my firm." She launched into a tale that now was quite entertaining but at the time felt like tough going for a new law graduate.

Georgia hadn't noticed Nev glancing at the doorway as she spoke. Then he beckoned another older man who entered the coffee shop. "Excuse me for interrupting, Georgia," he said, "but here's someone I'd like you to meet." Nev stood and shook the newcomer's hand. "Peter, I'd like you to meet Georgia. She's visiting us for a few days and was just telling us about some of her experiences as a lawyer in Sydney. Georgia, I'd like you to meet Peter O'Hara. Pete's our local solicitor and he's looking for a partner ahead of his retirement, once he knows where the fish are biting and when the weather's going to be good for a few games of golf."

As Georgia looked carefully into the shrewd eyes and kindly face of the man she'd just met, she knew. This was going to be her place. This would now be her home, her community.

Weekends

While I haven't really thought too much about it, every fortnight, my weekends always begin on Friday afternoon as soon as I arrive home from work. From my day job. The one that pays the small mortgage, the bills, the car expenses and adds, slightly, to my savings account. But every fortnight, when I sit with my cup of instant coffee and pour over bank statements, individual accounts, and my spreadsheet, I can see that I am managing much better than I'd ever hoped. And that was mainly because of the day job. My Monday-to-Friday, seven-to-three job managing the local supermarket.

It had been hard at first. But I'd really concentrated and put a lot of time, my time, here at home into working out staff shifts, designing displays, planning how to get the stock on the shelves as soon as humanly possible, and then trying to do all this with a genuine smile that welcomed my staff and our customers. All of them. The sweet, the sad, the silly, and the sour. Oh yes, we had them all in this little town. The gossipers. The groaners. The growlers. And once I'd become used to them, they all added to the enjoyment of my new job, and my new life.

Of course, it had taken time. Time for all of them and time for me. And, naturally, time for my boss, Joan McKinley. The town's wonder woman. Joan, widowed and in her mid-sixties, owned most of the commercial properties in this little town. The newsagency, managed by her niece and her husband, both in their forties with children attending the local high school, was hers. The pharmacy, managed by another newcomer like me to the little country town, an experienced Asian-Australian pharmacist in his mid-thirties and his equally qualified and experienced pharmacist wife, was also hers. The pharmacists' first child, a sweet, curly-headed girl, attended kindy and their second child was due in late September.

Joan's son was the local butcher and a regular place winner in the statewide best sausage maker competition. The year he'd won first prize, the pub, another of Joan's enterprises, had opened the bar to all local residents, with free soft drinks for kids and a non-alcoholic punch—her own recipe—for non-drinkers. While Joan didn't own the local hardware business or either of the two building companies based in the town, she did own a significant amount of the housing market. Joan's rental properties rarely changed tenants. She'd told me, during my interview for the position at the supermarket, that she didn't need to make big money out of her tenants. She wanted tenants that thought of their home as their home. If they cared for their home, then that made any ongoing maintenance easy and saved on property management costs. As well as many other great things in this community, Joan was a canny businesswoman.

And that suited me. I was qualified, my business degree proved that. I was experienced, too. Not only had I held a store and then district management position with one of Australia's major supermarkets, but my most recent management position was with one of the country's largest insurance companies. And the last three years I was there, I had slogged away at it until I knew, at last, I was done. I had nothing left in the engine. There was nothing left for me to give.

Thankfully, I had realised it before heading into a downward spiral like many other company mid-managers in similar positions. But the morning I'd pulled off the highway and parked, unplanned, in front of a local coffee shop, I knew it was over. "I don't want to do this anymore," I said aloud. Then I put my head on my hands that still gripped the steering wheel and breathed deeply. "I'm done."

Eventually, I was able to get out of the car and buy one of the coffees whose aroma had been tempting my nostrils from the moment I'd turned off the engine. Then, for the first time in eight months, I'd called in sick. Taking my coffee, and—yes, I'll admit it—a warm croissant across the road and into the welcoming sunlit park, I sat on a shady bench and watched the family of ducks paddling on the little creek that slowly meandered through the sloping grounds towards the wetlands about a mile and a half further along the highway. Despite the warning signs, I couldn't help myself and broke off some of the rich pastry and tossed it to the ducks. It made their day and helped make mine.

I handed in my resignation at the end of the week. That gave me a month to finish up and plan my future. Once I'd cleared out my desk and office, a task that took less than fifteen minutes, and attended the farewell morning tea and the after-work drinks, I was gone.

My first personal celebration of freedom was spending a week at home with my parents. That was easy—almost too easy. A week of being looked after, cared for, treated, and spoilt in the family home just out of Byron Bay was always enjoyable. While I'd planned to sleep late, the early summer sunrise seemed to beckon and I'd be up and walking along the beach, paddling and splashing through wavelets, breathing salty air, and soaking up sunshine. After just a few days, Mum told me I lost the pallor she'd been so worried about when I first arrived. Apparently, I'd been so pale and listless she and Dad had been concerned about my health.

My growing appetite had soon convinced them otherwise. And when the tan came back, they both knew I'd be okay. Yes, they had agreed, it was overwork. Overwork and stress. "And now you can stay here and relax with us; we'll look after you," they had said.

Letting them know I'd only be there for a week was almost as hard on me as it was for them. But once they knew of my plans to spend a month exploring Tasmania, they could see they had their adventure-loving daughter back. No longer was I the pale faced, city-based career woman they'd worried about. Their nature-loving girl was back, and so they could happily let me pack up and head off after our week of mutual indulgence.

That week with them and then the month I'd spent wandering—more than exploring—Tasmania had worked wonders. I was recharged, refreshed, and reinvigorated. And before I even had the time to wonder about what my next step might be, the advertisement for the supermarket manager's position in a country town caught my eye.

That's it, I thought, *that's me. I can do that. I'm probably over-qualified but what the hell. If they don't like my application or me then there'll be another job out there somewhere. But I like the look of this one,* I realised. Especially after I'd researched the town, its locality, and its population. Less than six hours away from Byron Bay, I knew Mum and Dad would love it, too. So I applied. And won.

And after eighteen busy months I had the satisfaction of knowing I'd been right. Yes, it had been a challenge at first. On all fronts. And then as I settled into the slower pace of working in a small town, of being responsible for the supermarket, its staff, the stock, anticipating the trends and seasonal demands of the customers, learning the suppliers and their travelling reps, I began to realise that this was a good fit for me. I soon started playing sport again. Netball in winter. I swam in summer. The local races and country music festival were part of my social calendar. And Mum and Dad came and stayed with me for these major events.

And then I began wanting more. At first, I wasn't sure just what it was that I wanted. Slowly, I narrowed it down. I tried hiking and bushwalking. Then I thought it might have been music, so I bought a guitar and took lessons. After three months, both my teacher and I were relieved when I decided that wasn't what I'd been looking for. Selling the just-broken-in guitar to one of her keen students was easy and another relief for me.

Then the high school's new contract art teacher offered evening lessons for adults. I was one of the first to sign up. Ten of us lined up at her garage studio for the first week's lesson. The next week there were fifteen of us. And over the next seven weeks, we all stuck to it. The wine, cheese, and biscuits probably helped, because we weren't the most talented artists in town, but it was fun. A lot of fun and a lot of creativity. And that's what led me to what I was seeking. If, three years earlier, I'd been told that I'd spend my evenings creating scented candles, I would have laughed. Long and loud. But early on, in the art teacher's garage studio, when we were all talking about our interests, artistic and otherwise, the idea of scented candles popped into my head and wouldn't go away. I talked about it with Beth, the art teacher, when everyone else had cleaned up and gone home.

"Look into it, Crystal," she advised. "Okay, you don't know where the idea's come from; that doesn't matter. At the very least, you have to honour the idea."

Yes, Beth was a bit New Agey or in tune with her inner self or whatever the terms for this kind of thing are. Having been deeply immersed in the city career cycle, I certainly wasn't up with New Age, self-care, free-thinking, spiritualistic terminology, or anything else that had been evolving outside my own previous narrow focus.

"Research candles, candle making, the cottage industry, and see just what's needed," Beth advised. "Do some market research; your background will be a strength for that. Find out about courses or kits or whatever's needed. Go to the library—see what resources they have or what they're able to get in for you. Follow the thought. It might lead you nowhere or it might lead you to something else, but don't let it shrivel and die. The idea has come to you for a reason; nurture it and see what happens."

And then at the end of the semester, Beth and her evening art classes were gone. Thankfully, due to technology, she wasn't totally removed from my creative endeavours. We'd catch up by Zoom every three or four weeks, and I'd call her my artistic mentor. Part of our session was dedicated to creativity and how I was progressing, then we'd focus on her contract work and wherever it took her, and then we'd chat about music, recipes, and fashion, and our friendship continued to grow.

As did my candle-making endeavours. It was hard. It was more work than I'd anticipated. But it was also more enjoyable than I'd anticipated. And one weekend, when I was finally happy with my latest results, I'd excitedly boxed up the best of the batch and sent them off to Mum and Dad with instructions to share them out amongst the family, friends, and neighbours.

I didn't anticipate their response to this, though. Oh, no—Mum and Dad weren't giving their little girl's hard work away to anyone. They approached their local gift shops, newsagents, pharmacies, florists—anyone and everyone—presenting them with an introductory offer to a new, exciting range of Outback Australian Handmade Candles, that, apparently, they'd be mad to miss out on.

Suddenly, and unexpectedly, the first real orders arrived. Mum rang, full of excitement. "Crystal, darling, how many of those dear little candles do you have? Right now?" she asked.

"Right now? Oh, about twenty, I think, Mum. Why?""Good, pack them up and send them tomorrow, darling. We've got two orders for a dozen each. I'll give a dozen to Cheryl at the newsagents and the other eight to Barry at the information centre. I'll let him know that you'll send more by the end of the week. You can do that, can't you?"

"What? What do you mean, orders?"

"Oh, your father and I decided we weren't giving them away, darling. We took them all over town and some places have sold out. You'll need to make more, lots more, as soon as you can," she replied. "Now," she continued, "your most popular ones are the lemon myrtle and the lavender, but the vanilla and pear fragrance blend isn't far behind. And maybe you can make some bigger sizes—what do you think? You can do that, can't you?"

"Whoa, whoa, whoa, Mum. Slow down. What's going on? What do you mean orders? Bigger sizes? Just what have you and Dad done?"

And as she explained, my excitement grew. While part of me was just a little bit cross that they'd put my work out for public sale without me knowing, a bigger part was amazed and then thankful that they had. And another part of me was jumping up and down with pride.

"Oh boy, Mum, Dad. This is big. This is right out of the blue. So, you're telling me that some of my candles have been sold? For money?"

In the background, I could hear Dad laughing. "Yes, Crystal, for money. We have about two hundred and forty dollars here for you. Nineteen of those candles you sent us were sold for eighteen dollars each, with the shopkeepers taking six dollars per candle. We thought that'd be okay with you, because you'd asked us to just give them away. As soon as your mum lit the first one, we knew that we couldn't hand them out willy-nilly. You're onto something here, darling, so send us those others as soon as you can, will you? Now, you'll have to get an ABN and set up a sales and invoicing system, and a profit and loss recording system, so we thought we'd head out next week and give you a hand with all that so you can just keep on making them in whatever spare time you have. How's that sound?"

"Wow, Dad, I can hardly keep up with you. I'm going to need time to really get my head around this. Yes, please come out next week. Whatever it is you've just said hasn't sunk in yet. And it sounds like I'll be busy packaging tonight to get them to the post office tomorrow. Oh boy, I'll need time to catch up with you two. You don't let the grass grow, do you?" I smiled into the phone, my mind racing as I tried to process all that had happened without my knowledge.

And now, just a short three months later, it was still happening. Every second Friday night, I'd pack the car and have it ready for a very early morning start. Then on the first Saturday morning of the month, I'd set up my candle stall at the local market in the park on the riverbank. Usually, most of the stock would be gone and orders taken well before the market officially finished. Being able to pack up and leave almost two hours before some of the other stall holders added to my happiness as the early knock-off added time to my weekend.

A fortnight later, I'd head off very early to the Saturday market in the next town an hour or so along the highway. Again, I'd sell out early, take orders, and then socialise with other stall holders and regular customers. And it was here, one busy Saturday morning, that I met Mark. He'd wanted a collection of nice candles for his mum for her birthday and we'd started chatting. As there were only ten candles left for sale, he didn't have a huge choice, but he bought three and I'd arranged them on a small pottery plate and gift-wrapped them in clear cellophane tied with a pretty floral ribbon.

I hadn't expected to see him again. But after taking them to his car, he'd hovered nearby and saw the last of my stock being sold. He watched as I started packing up the table and canopy and came back to help and asked if I'd like to have a coffee with him. Coffee turned into lunch. By the time I had to leave and drive home, we'd arranged for him to drive up the highway and meet me again for lunch the next day.

We're still sorting this out. But each Saturday morning Mark travels up the highway to spend the weekend with me. Then when it's time for me to take my ever-growing range of scented candles to the market in his town, I pack up Friday afternoon to set off early Saturday morning and drive along the highway that we're both getting to know so very well.

Vale Joe

Louise, the registered nurse on duty, gently removed her fingers from the now-still carotid artery as she looked at the time on her fob watch. Carefully observing the old man's chest, she knew she'd been there for him as he'd exhaled his last breath. Drawing in a deep breath of her own, she noted the final details on the clipboard chart and looked up as the doctor quietly slipped through the cubicle's closed curtains.

"He's gone," she said softly. "Just a minute and a half ago."

The young doctor nodded, his eyes full of compassion. "I'll start the arrangements," he said. "When you've finished here, have a break, make a cuppa, talk to someone, come back and talk to me if you like, but have a break. This has been hard for all of us." Louise nodded as she tried to smile through her tears. "Thanks, Alex. I'll do that. I am okay … sort of. I'll make sure the right people know first; they'll know what to do next, I suppose." She looked down at the frail old body. "Travel gently, Joe. Peace be with you now and for your eternal sleep." She lightly kissed her fingers and touched them to his cheek.

"He's no-one's; he's everyone's. The town will mourn him. We'll all look after him." With a sad smile at the new doctor the community had quickly come to like and respect, she gently eased through the curtains and quietly left the room.

Drawing warmth from her mug of tea, Louise sat at the nurses' station desk and picked up the phone. Checking the number to make sure she connected to the right person first, she listened as it rang and was then answered.

"Morning; Nev speaking."

"Nev, it's Louise from the hospital. Just ringing to let you know Joe passed away about ten minutes ago. It was quiet and peaceful. I held his hand. He knew someone was with him as he drifted away." She heard the sob in her voice and took another deep breath.

"You were the one he asked us to let know first. I am sorry, Nev. He thought the world of you and the gang. He loved hearing your stories over and over again. Alex is with him now." She paused.

"I'll be there in ten, Louise. I'd like to see him before he has to leave his room. It's still early yet; there's no rush to move him, is there?"

"No, Nev. See you soon, I'll let Alex know you're coming.

The word of Joe's passing travelled quickly around the community. Sadness was its companion as phone after phone rang with the news. The council foreman didn't wait to be told as he raised the flag to half-mast outside the civic centre. The small primary and secondary schools followed suit as did the bowls club, the golf club, and all other organisations with a flag and a pole. The few private homes with flagpoles also showed their respect to Joe's passing with lowered flags.

Flowers were placed at Joe's favourite seat outside the small supermarket where he'd sit and yarn with old and young alike. Crystal, the supermarket manager, asked the staff to make sure the flowers looked as fresh as possible. "Spray them with water every half-hour or so, please. They'll wilt soon enough, but if we can keep them looking good that might help anyone who sits there with their memories. By God, he'll be missed around here." Her eyes shone with tears as she looked around her staff. All were emotional— she knew they would be and so would the town. "I'll check with Joan," she told them. "If she's happy, we'll close for his service, then I'll come back and open up. I'm sure she won't mind. That way you'll all be able to stay and pay your respects. Joe'd like that, I think."

"He would, Crystal, and I'm sure Joan won't mind. I reckon just about everyone will be there; maybe not the schoolkids and teachers, but just about everyone else, I reckon." Crystal nodded at Theo, the young school-leaver who worked as trolley boy, shelf stacker, check-out operator, deli server, and bag carrier and did anything else that needed doing.

"Think you're right, Theo," she murmured. "We've all known this was coming, but it doesn't make it any easier. Have a think about what you'd all like to do, either at his service as a recognition from all of us or after. I've got a couple of ideas, but I don't think this is the right time for them." She looked up as the automatic doors slid open.

"Joan, how are you?" she asked the owner of the supermarket as well as a good number of the town's other businesses. "I'll make you a coffee if you've got time."

"Thanks, Crystal, that'd be great," the older woman said. "Nev's just let me know Joe's service is Thursday morning. We'll all be closing a bit after half-past nine. The civic centre will be packed, so there'll be sound speakers outside, seats, a marquee, and a couple of gazebos for shade. Nev and Shirley from the CWA are planning the service and the details. Joe's burial arrangements are underway and a small group of us have been asked to call into Peter O'Hara's this afternoon. Not sure why the solicitor wants to see us, but s'pose we'll find out then. Now," she continued, nodding her thanks to Crystal as she took hold of the coffee mug, "people will want to talk. They'll be talking everywhere. Try not to let them hold you up too much; make sure you get them through the checkouts fairly quickly, and I know none of you, especially you Crystal, need me telling you what to do and how to do it, but dear old Joe, he was no-one's, but he was everyone's. We all looked out for him, we all took care of him one way or another, and we're all going to be sad. All of us. My little neighbour, Sonia, saw me on her way to day care this morning and said she was sorry Joe had died and she gave me a big hug. Told me she knew I loved him and helped look after him. When kids that little know what's going on around them, then it shows what a great community we have here.

"Thanks, Crystal," she said as she handed back the half-empty mug. "I needed that. Okay, I've got to go. Take care, everyone—of yourselves and each other. Talk when you need to, cry when you need to, but don't wallow. We all know Joe wouldn't want that." With a sniff, her eyes blinking back tears, Joan smiled and turned to leave. "Just a moment, Joan," Crystal found herself saying. "Take this with you."

She reached out and, for the first time ever, hugged the woman who'd employed her. Holding her close, Crystal murmured, "That little kid was right—you loved Joe, you looked after him, you cared for him. You look after yourself, too, right?"

The air felt heavy, Crystal thought as she locked the supermarket shortly after nine-thirty Thursday morning. *There's sadness in the air*, she realised as she looked around the empty street. Two cars were parked at the far end of the street—*Overflow from around the civic centre*, she thought as she walked briskly along the town's main street.

Even though she'd expected a crowd, Crystal was surprised by the huge number of people outside the venue. The street had been cordoned off and people were sitting along it, facing the civic centre with two large speakers positioned either side of the steps leading to its entrance. She found a seat with others she knew and waited for Joe's service to begin. Soon, Nev's well-known voice came through the speakers as he outlined the order of service.

As Joe had no family, Nev had asked a number of people to share their memories of the town's well-known character. Peter O'Hara, the local solicitor, was the first speaker and what he had to say surprised almost everyone there. "We all knew Joe," he began. "But not many of us knew Joe well. Yes, we knew he was a returned serviceman, he served in Africa, Palestine, and New Guinea. Like so many others, he suffered during and after his service. But Joe made peace with that. We'd watch and applaud him in our Anzac Day parade, and we'd see him at the Remembrance Day ceremony. To those who spoke to him on those occasions, Joe asked me to say thank you. Your recognition meant a lot to him. Joe loved this town," Peter continued. "He loved the town and its people. He appreciated the way everyone looked out for him. He greatly appreciated the care he received over the last few months of his life. He did not expect this many people here today and he would be very surprised but also very pleased to see just who is here. Seeing the primary and secondary school captains and other children from both schools would have brought that great, big smile to his face. Joe decided that he wanted to leave a legacy for the kids of this town. A lasting legacy, not necessarily with his name, but something that would be useful and fun for the kids. And Joe knew that kids love water—being in it, playing with it, splashing it. So, a couple of months ago, he asked me to make a quiet representation to the local council on his behalf. Today, I'm proud to announce that the council agreed to Joe's proposal to build a water playground at the pool. Joe has fully funded the water playground and the council is happy to provide its ongoing maintenance and upkeep as an activity for our local children." Peter smiled as those gathered gasped, whispered, and then applauded. He held his hands up when people started to stand.

"No, not yet," he advised. "Joe has more to give; I have more to tell you. In Joe's name, there will be ongoing annual bursaries for our primary and secondary school students. These will include academic, sporting and athletic, music and artistic, and speech and drama bursaries for girls and boys." Again, he held up his hands as people started to applaud.

"For students who finish their schooling here and enrol in further tertiary study out of town, there will be a first-year grant in two payments: one at the start of the year and the second at the start of second semester. This, Joe hoped, will help them settle into unfamiliar places and their new studies." Again, Peter's hand went up.

"Finally, there is a bequest to our aged care facility, a place Joe never intended going to but a place he knew was needed and a place that he respected for being there for those older than him and, in a few cases, those his age and younger. Joe loved this town and this community. He knew you cared for him when you didn't have to. He had the means to look after himself and to do that well. But he loved your interactions with him. This is his way of thanking everyone: the children, the students, our young people, and our older people. Joe knew there'd be a few people who'd want to say a few words here today, but he wanted me to go first. I'll now step aside and hand back to Nev. Vale, Joe. Rest peacefully." Peter left the lectern to a standing ovation that everyone knew was just for Joe.

The community farewelled the man they'd called their own in their own way. Stories were told—most were true, some were far-fetched. Some were happy, some were compassionately sad. All were sincere.

And, at the end of that year, when summer came, the new Mister Joe's Water Playground facility, named by the town's children, was declared open and the water flowed. Students from the primary and secondary schools received bursaries for the coming school year's books, shoes, and uniforms—with books and stationery being the priority. The high school's graduates, enrolling and planning their tertiary studies, received notification of their grants for when they'd leave their community, and the first sods of the Joe Burke Activity Centre at the aged care facility were turned over by Joan, Nev, and Peter O'Hara in front of a large crowd of onlookers.

To the Reader

Thank you for reading *Sense of Place: Stories about Community and Belonging.* I hope you've enjoyed them.

The regional town in which these stories are set is not one specific town. It is best described as an amalgamation of places I have been lucky enough to live in, work in, or visit and stay in more than once, over many years of travelling.

Last year, inspiration seemed to arrive with my coffee when I attended the 2023 Words Out West Festival. I felt as if I was watching Dalby's central business district wake up and ready itself for a new day and began writing words, sentences, thoughts, and ideas on my serviette. A week later, the first draft of the first story came out of my printer and the idea for this collection began to grow.

Just as the setting is not one specific town, the Take-a-Break Café has come from many of the coffee shops, bakeries, and cafés I have frequented over the years.

From Brighton and Black Rock in Melbourne to Echuca and Moama on the River Murray, Deniliquin, Jerilderie, and other stopping places along the Newell Highway, the delights of Stanthorpe, Warwick, Moree, Bourke, and St George, as well as my Friday breakfasts in Acacia Ridge, and my regular haunts in Beaudesert—the sense of place and community that each of these coffee shops offers regular customers and visitors has provided the inspiration for the central gathering place in some of these stories.

Importantly, not one of the characters in any of these stories is real. When you've walked the earth as long as I have, many unique people have moved in and out of my personal orbit, creating and leaving a smorgasbord of memories, images, and feelings that have fed my imagination. For this, while I am thankful, I am unable to identify any single person who has jumped from my pen onto any of these pages. If, for whatever reason, you feel a connection to any of the characters inside these covers, I hope you see it as a coincidence and a compliment.

www.ingramcontent.com/pod-product-compliance
Lightning Source LLC
Chambersburg PA
CBHW071014180726
48291CB00004B/1457